THE HOUSE IN HIDING

THE HOUSE IN HIDING

ELINOR LYON

CANONGATE · KELPIES

First published in 1950 by Hodder and Stoughton
First published by Canongate Kelpies in 1991

Text © Elinor Lyon 1950

Printed and bound in Great Britain by
Cox and Wyman, Reading

ISBN 0 86241 338 9

CANONGATE PRESS PLC
14 FREDERICK STREET,
EDINBURGH EH2 2HB, SCOTLAND

CONTENTS

Chapter				*Page*
1.	THE CHILDREN WHO COULDN'T	.	.	7
2.	BURNING DOWN THE BOTHY	.	.	26
3.	ESCAPE AND DISCOVERY	.	.	37
4.	THE SECRET SHIELING	.	.	66
5.	A CHASE AND A RESCUE	.	.	81
6.	THE HEIR OF KINDRACHILL	.	.	97
7.	ANN IS A NUISANCE	.	.	109
8.	FOUR BOOTS AND A MOUNTAIN	.	.	128
9.	A PERILOUS VOYAGE	.	.	143
10.	MYSTERIOUS VISITORS	.	.	163
11.	THE RETURN OF THE CHIEFTAIN	.	.	181
12.	TREASURE ON THE ISLAND	.	.	195
13.	WELCOME HOME	.	.	217

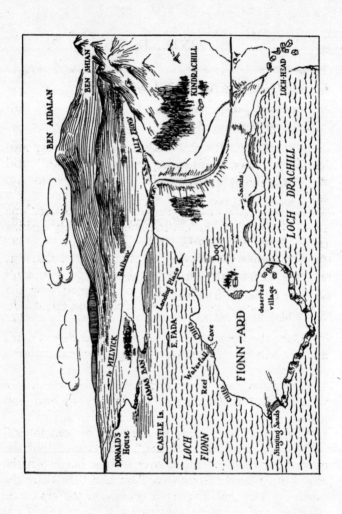

1. The Children who Couldn't

"I'M GLAD I'M ALIVE, AND looking at Skye, and eating marmalade tart," said the boy sitting on the hillside. "I might easily not be."

His sister, lying on the grass beside him, opened one eye and looked at him, then shut it quickly against the brightness of the sky.

"If I hadn't shoved you out of the way of that car, you wouldn't be any of them," she said. "You can't go dreaming along the middle of the road now the holiday season's begun, not even in the West Highlands. You ought to know that."

"Och, there wasn't any danger. And anyway, it's not August yet. That's when you get the real crowd of trippers."

"Do hurry with that tart," said the girl. "I've finished mine and it makes me hungry to hear you eating."

"Och, shut up. Look at the view or something."

"I know the view by heart," she retorted, but she opened her eyes and rolled over to look out across the sound to where the islands lay hazy and blue along the horizon. The sea shimmered quietly in the afternoon sunshine, and even the waves on the shore just below had lost their noise and fury, and stumbled sleepily up the banks of orange shells and seaweed to the tide-mark of foam.

" I do hope this weather lasts," said the boy. " It's just perfect for rowing round the loch."

" If we get the boat there'll probably be a hurricane or a tidal wave straight away."

" And we may not get it, you know. I wish Daddy would hurry up in there."

They looked down at the small house on the coast road just below. Their father, Dr. Kennedy, was in there attending to a bad leg, and the man who owned the bad leg also owned a boat, which the doctor had promised he would try to hire for his family.

" If we do get it," said the girl, " let's try and get to Castle Island. It would take ages, but we could do it if we had the whole day."

" It's funny that we've never managed to reach it, when it's been sitting out there looking at us all our lives. I don't think we ever will get there," said the boy. " Talking of boats, did you know there was a saint who sailed about in a coracle made out of stone ? "

" No," said his sister. " He would. There's Daddy, look ! "

She leapt to her feet and ran down the steep grassy slope towards the road, as the doctor appeared at the door of the cottage. He had to stoop to get through the doorway, for he was a very tall man.

" Daddy ! Did you ask him ? " cried his daughter, racing towards him with her black hair flying out behind her. The boy was close at her heels, and together they flung themselves breathlessly at Dr. Kennedy.

" Of course I asked him about the boat," said the doctor patiently. " Haven't you been pestering me about it regularly every ten minutes since breakfast? Would my life be worth living if I hadn't asked Donald about his boat? Do you suppose I've been allowed to forget about Donald and his boat for one moment of the day?"

" Oh, stop it," exclaimed the girl. " Did you get it?"

" Was he willing to hire it out?" asked the boy.

" Yes he was, but I haven't hired it."

" What?"

" I've bought it. I thought it would be cheaper in the end, instead of having to buy him a new boat when you've sunk this one or run it on the rocks."

" Oh, we wouldn't!"

" I bet you would if you got the chance. I wouldn't let you near a boat if I didn't know you could both swim quite well."

" You've bought it for us?" repeated the boy, a little dazed by the thought of suddenly owning a boat.

" Yes. Donald owed me more than it's worth, but I took it in return for all the liniment and good advice I've bestowed on him. Go along and look at it. I've got to get on my way; there are some flourishing measles waiting for me in Melvick."

" Poor Daddy," said his daughter. " You don't get much of a holiday season."

" Oh, it makes a change. Frostbite and pneumonia

all winter, and digging fish-hooks out of visitors' arms all summer. Well, go and find your boat. Can you row it home by yourselves ? "

" Och, yes. We'll have the tide with us, and there's no wind," said the girl confidently.

" And it doesn't get dark till eleven," said the boy.

" All right," said their father. " Be careful, now. Ian, you're the eldest. See that Sovra doesn't get drowned. Sovra, you've got more sense than Ian. See he doesn't do anything stupid. Good-bye."

He strode off towards his car, which he had left on the side of the road.

They stood and looked at each other excitedly. They were both brown and thin and black-haired and plain. They both wore cotton shirts and old khaki shorts and sandshoes ; Ian had a hole where his right big toe poked through, Sovra had a hole for her left one. These were their holiday clothes. School had ended for both of them the day before, and was already forgotten, drowned in the blaze of the sun and shimmer of the water.

" Come on," said Sovra, and started running down towards the shore. Ian followed more slowly, thinking about the boat made of stone. After all, you can get thousands of tons of iron to float quite easily ; why not stone ?

The boat was lying on one side, pulled up on the pebble beach below the cottage, in a little bay sheltered by rocks. It was not a large boat, but it looked wide and shallow-built and difficult to overturn. Old Donald had used it for fishing before his bad leg got too much for him, and they had often seen him setting out in the evening with two rods propped against the thwarts and the two lines running out behind the boat. When a rod jerked, Donald let his oars rest in the rowlocks, leaned forward and reeled in the fish, then paid out the line as the boat drifted and started rowing again, all without getting up from his seat. Ian and Sovra had longed to try it, it looked so easy.

" We must go fishing soon by ourselves," said Sovra, as Ian joined her by the boat. They had been out after mackerel and saith, but always in somebody else's boat.

" Perhaps we'd better get it into the water first," suggested Ian.

" Silly ! We'll have to do some baling first. The floorboards would be awash if it wasn't so much on its side."

There were two empty tins in the boat, which had been used to bale it out before, and they set to work with these.

" I suppose this is the last lot of rain," said Sovra. " I'd have thought it'd dry up in this weather."

" It's had the whole year's rain in it," Ian pointed out. " It's a good thing, too."

" Why ? "

" If it was quite dry, the boards would shrink, and it might leak badly until they were wet enough to swell again. As it is, that upper side looks rather dry."

" I hope we don't sink it. Daddy thinks we always make a mess of things."

" Well, so we do, usually. But we don't when we are in a boat."

" At any rate," said Sovra severely, " we won't be getting run over by cars."

" We'll probably get rammed by motor-boats instead. I think that's good enough," said Ian, putting the tin under the stern seat. There was still a little water there but not enough to cover the floor-boards when they pulled the boat upright on its keel.

" Oh, isn't this thrilling ! " Sovra exclaimed. " Come on, let's push it down."

The tide was nearly high, and with the help of two round pieces of wood that Donald had left for rollers they managed to trundle the boat down and into the water. As soon as it was afloat Ian pushed off, and they both scrambled in over the stern.

Ian looked out at the shining waters of the loch, and westwards to the open sea, where perhaps they could venture now by themselves. He was feeling much too adventurous and excited to notice a bubbling rush of water spurting up by his feet, even when it surged over his shoes. Sovra looked down and found the sea coming in through a large round hole, and the boat sinking lower and lower in the water.

" Look out ! " she cried.   " Ian, we're sinking ! "

" My sorrow," said Ian, looking calmly at the water washing round his ankles. " We never put the bung in the bung-hole."

" Oh, stop talking and get out ! " Sovra was already over the side and knee-deep beside the boat, trying to pull it back to the shore. Ian clambered out and helped her, and after a struggle they beached the boat again and looked at each other across half a boatful of water.

"I'm glad Daddy didn't see that," said Sovra. "Come on, we'll have to bale again. My baling muscles are stiff already."

"We'll have to find the bung," said Ian. "I bet old Donald's got it all the time."

"Go and ask him. I'll bale."

"Why don't you go and ask him? He thinks I'm daft enough as it is, but he treats you as if you had sense, I can't think why."

"No, you go," said Sovra, baling hard. "Men always do the asking people for things. Women just do the work."

"Oh, all right," said her brother. He always found it easier to give in than to argue.

Sovra thought about the boat as she went on baling. They would have to find a name for it. They might even give it another coat of paint if they ever had any money to spare. The white paint on it now was cracked and flaking off. There was a big stone in the bows, with a rope tied round it and coiled neatly in a pile, its other end attached to a ring.

"That's for an anchor," said Sovra to herself. She liked being able to look at things in a leisurely way and note the details.

There were footsteps on the sliding pebbles behind her, and she turned to see Ian approaching, carrying two oars over his shoulder, and red to his collar-bones.

"That old man," he said resentfully, putting the

oars in the boat. "He knew we'd forget about the bung, and when he saw my wet feet he just roared with laughter. And then he said if we wanted to get home to-night we'd best take the oars. Did you think about oars? I didn't."

"We would have, if the boat hadn't started sinking. But I'm glad he can't come out and watch us. We'd probably find we were going backwards or something. Have you got the bung?"

Ian took a round wooden plug from his pocket, and fitted it into the hole in the bottom of the boat, hammering it tight with a stone.

"Now, is there anything else we've forgotten?" he asked.

"Rowlocks? No, they're in already. And we've got an anchor, look. I think we're all right now."

They pushed the boat into the water again, and embarked rather cautiously, but it floated out like a bird, heaving a little as the subdued waves swelled beneath it. Ian disentangled the oars, which had somehow got mixed up with the anchor rope and the baling tins and his own feet, and set them in the rowlocks.

"I hope we're going to manage all right," said Sovra, watching him rather doubtfully.

"I'm all right once I get going," said Ian. "You'd better be careful, though."

"Of course. I always am," said Sovra, and immediately knocked an oar overboard. By the time she had rescued it and put it back in the rowlock she felt hot and flustered.

" I'll row," said Ian, " I've done it oftener than you. Will you guide me ? "

She nodded, and clambered forward into the bows. The mooring rope coiled there made a knobbly sort of seat, and by leaning forward she could look down through the clear water and see the pebbles and boulders and waving weed fathoms below.

Ian took the oars and felt competent again. He had often rowed in other people's boats, and in a few minutes he had remembered the slow sweep and pull that his father had taught him years ago. The boat responded to his strokes, and began to move diagonally away from the shore. Donald's house stood just where the sea-loch broadened into the Hebridean sound, and the Kennedy's house lay on the shore of the loch some miles further inland. The children had to row along the coast until they reached Camas Ban, the white bay, where a burn ran down past their house into the loch. As the boat moved away from the shore, the islands sailed into sight ; blue crags and precipice peaks, shining rock and dusky shadow, stretching far and dim. In this fine weather they were faint as clouds. When rain was threatening they would stand out bold and black, but as the rain blew over them they gradually vanished in the mist, so that it was difficult to believe they were real islands at all.

The hills of the mainland were clearer than the islands, though a sunny haze lay on them too, and Loch Fionn looked like a finger that the sea had pushed in between them. The boat was heading for the range of higher hills where the loch ended. Among these rose a black peak of scowling rock—Ben Shian, the highest mountain in sight.

The next finger of sea was Loch Drachill, and between the two lochs lay Fionn-ard, a narrow headland where nobody ever went. People said there was nothing there worth seeing, but Ian and Sovra had never been able to get there to find out. If you came from the mainland you were stopped by a bog, and if you came by boat there was nowhere to land because of the cliffs. The railway cut straight across the neck of the headland from Lochhead, the village at the end of Loch Drachill, then rounded the head of Loch Fionn on a big viaduct and turned west towards Melvick. The road ran beside it, and Ian and Sovra knew every inch of it, from their house up round the loch, under the viaduct, past a big empty house and into Lochhead, but they knew nothing about Fionn-ard because they had never been there.

It was so warm and quiet in their boat that they were not thinking about Fionn-ard or even Castle Island.

Ian gazed out to sea as he rowed, and Donald's house grew smaller and smaller until it merged in the blurred green and grey of the shore. The sun made a shimmer and dazzle on the surface of the water, and he half-shut his eyes, so that the blue water and blue islands swam together in the rainbow criss-cross of his eyelashes. Sovra, behind him, was leaning over the bows as far as she dared, watching the rays of light slant down through the water. Sometimes they lit up a floating bunch of seaweed, sometimes there was a silver gleam as a fish sped across the boat's path, but most of the time there was nothing to be seen beyond the dark depths.

Suddenly Sovra saw rocks, rising from the gloom, ribbed and weedy and threatening. She cried out in alarm, for Ian was rowing straight at them.

" A reef ! " she shouted. " Back water hard ! "

Ian started violently, and looked round, threshing the water in his attempt to check the boat. There was the reef, breaking the surface only a few yards ahead ; a long low rock with unpleasant sharp edges.

The oars waved fiercely amid showers of spray, and the boat heaved and shuddered and slewed round just in time. Sovra leaned out and pushed the boat away as they came within reach of the rock. Something scraped along the hull, there was one awful moment when the boat jerked sideways and shipped some water over the side, and then they were out in clear water, breathless and safe.

Ian leaned on the oars and panted, while Sovra gazed wildly around her.

" Where have we got to ? " she exclaimed. " I can't see any place I know."

" We've not been out as far as this before," said Ian, when he had recovered enough to look about him. " It looks different, but it's still the same loch, if you see what I mean."

" Of course it is," she replied impatiently. " But where are we ? "

" Halfway across Loch Fionn. I thought you said you'd guide me."

" Oh. So I did. Och, well, we might as well explore, now we are here."

They soon got their bearings, and could tell exactly where they were. The reef they had just escaped lay about halfway between Camas Ban and the shore of Fionn-ard, beyond the usual routes for fishing boats. The loch was full of islands, and Sovra recited their names as she recognised them. Castle Island was further out to westward. Its real name was Eilean Glas, which was a dull name meaning Grey Island. They preferred to call it Castle Island, because of the square lump of rock that crowned it.

" We *will* go there one day," Sovra declared.

" Will we go there, too ? " suggested Ian, turning to look at Fionn-ard. They had never seen it so close before. The shore was one unbroken cliff, feathered with twisted birches and rowans and tufted with heather. There were waves foaming against the foot of the outer-most point, the only waves in all that quiet sea. Above the cliff the hills rose steep and green, not very high but big enough to hide whatever lay inland.

" There's no landing place," said Sovra. " The waves are making a lot of noise, aren't they ? "

" It's not the waves," said Ian. " It's that waterfall."

Sovra looked where he was pointing, and exclaimed in surprise. A white column of water arched out from the top of the cliff and thundered into the sea, churning it into a foaming whirlpool. There was a sunny mist about the waterfall where the light fell on the spray, and some seagulls were swooping down and round and up again, as white as the foam.

"You can see it from the train," said Sovra. "I've often noticed it, but I never realized it was so big."

"You know, it's not a bad thing to be stupid sometimes," reflected Ian. "If you'd guided me the shortest way home, we'd not have seen Fionn-ard close to, and we'd have missed the waterfall. I wish we could get closer."

"We can try some time. I suppose we ought to go home now. If Daddy tells Mummy what we're doing she'll be worried. She thinks we're much stupider than we are."

"The tide's coming in still," Ian remarked. They had drifted some way up the loch while they looked at Fionn-ard, and were by now opposite the waterfall.

"Doesn't the water look streaky! I suppose there are all sorts of queer currents up this side of the loch, what with reefs and waterfalls and things. I say, we'd better start rowing, Ian. Just look at the way the shore's racing along."

The boat had drifted into the current that scoured the foot of the cliff, and it seemed as though the whole of Fionn-ard were gliding smoothly past.

"Let me take one oar," Sovra suggested, climbing over the pile of rope coils. Ian moved one of the row-locks and gave her an oar, and they started to turn the boat out of the current.

"Tell me if I'm not rowing fast enough," said Sovra. "Isn't there a song about 'Hurrah for the homeward bound'?"

"We're bounding rather un-homeward just now. We're miles past the reef."

" Well, get a move on then, instead of making feeble jokes. Let's go straight across to Eilean Fada."

" I hope there aren't any more reefs," said Ian, looking over his shoulder as he rowed. " That one's nearly covered now. There's seaweed all over it, so I suppose it's right under water at high tide."

" Once we're past Eilean Fada it will be all right. You can make straight for home from there and no reefs at all."

This island, a long shelf of grey rock scrubby with heather and rough grass, lay a hundred yards or so ahead, and as the boat drew slowly level with it the rowers found their work easier.

" The island's keeping off the tide," said Ian.

" And the wind. The water's all rippled over there."

" It's queer the way there's always a wee bit of wind coming in with the tide. There was none at all just now. Perhaps the water draws the air with it. . . ."

He went on murmuring to himself, and Sovra in front of him suddenly found the rowing much harder.

" We're going round in circles," she said. " Are we in a whirlpool ? "

" I don't think so," said Ian absently. She looked round and saw that he was resting idly on his oar, gazing at the horizon with dreamy blue eyes.

" *Ian !* You're not rowing. Of course we're going round. Wake up, do."

He smiled kindly at her, and started to row again, remarking,

" I wonder if it's exactly twelve miles you can see along the level of the water. To the skyline, I mean."

" Who says it is ? "

" Och, I don't know.   I read it somewhere."

" Does it matter ? "

" It might.   You never know."

" If you were as clever as you think you are," she said severely, " we'd be home and having our tea at this moment, instead of havering about like a lost snipe."

" Come on then," said Ian, and they bent to the oars so vigorously that Eilean Fada was soon far behind them, and they were in sight of the opening of Camas Ban. It was a narrow inlet, sheltered on either side by high rocks which made it a safe harbour for a boat.   Ian took both oars as they entered the calm water of the bay, and pulled slowly for the shore.   Sovra hoisted the anchor stone on to the edge of the boat, ready to heave it out.

" Fairly soon," said Ian, glancing behind him. " The tide's nearly high and we don't want the boat too far up the beach.   Now ! "

Sovra pushed the stone over, and it vanished with a thunderous splash, the coiled rope flickering after it.   Ian stopped rowing, and the boat drifted in as far as the anchor rope allowed, coming to rest beside a low spur of rock running out from the shore.

" Rather neat, don't you think ? " he remarked, laying hold of the rock.   " I wish Daddy had seen that."

" Be careful.   We're not on dry land yet."

They scrambled out onto the rock with caution, and gained the shore without any mishap, bringing with them the free end of the mooring rope.   This they

knotted round a large boulder, pulling the boat a little
sideways so that it lay in clear water away from the
rocks.

"Doesn't she look lovely," said Sovra. The water
was so still, in spite of the little burn running into it,
that the boat was reflected as clear as life and nearly as
bright, with the shimmer of the blue sky all round and
below its weatherbeaten whiteness. The rope dipping
into the water had another rope rising to meet it from
the reflected bows.

They left the boat in its loveliness and ran home
across the white sand and shells and pebbles. They
felt full of gratitude towards their father, and as soon
as the house was in sight they saw him sitting on the
doorstep rubbing at his fishing boots. He was having
a loud conversation with someone indoors, presumably
Mrs. Kennedy getting tea ready. As the children
approached they heard him shout,

"I tell you there's not a room to be had. I've tried
every hotel for miles. They'll have to come here.
You can get a girl in to help."

Faint expostulations came from inside, and he turned
round to reply,

"They'll have the children's rooms, of course."

"Where will *they* sleep?" demanded the distant
voice.

"In the bothy. Why not?"

"Supposing it rains?"

"Of course it'll rain. Doesn't it rain all the time
when it's not snowing? Haven't you heard that remark
about the Isle of Skye—' When you can see it clear it's

going to rain ; when you can't see it, it is raining ' ? The bothy will keep out the rain."

Ian and Sovra looked at each other with wide eyes, wondering what on earth their parents were talking about. The ' bothy ' was a hut that stood behind the house, and on very fine nights in summer they were allowed to camp out there and cook their supper romantically out of doors. Their mother said the place was damp and the food got sooty, which was true but not important. Dr. Kennedy said that modern children ought to be taught to rough it, but he had never before suggested that they should sleep there whatever the weather.

He looked up as they approached, and said,

" So you're not drowned."

" Oh, Daddy, the boat's wonderful ! " cried Sovra. " You *are* nice to get it for us."

Ian nodded enthusiastically to show that he agreed, and their father laughed.

" Anything to get you off the roads. You ought to be safe in a boat by now."

" What were you saying about the bothy ? " demanded Sovra.

" I believe I said it would keep out the rain. Ask your mother what she thinks."

" Yes, but why ? Who's going to sleep in our rooms ? Why have you been trying every hotel for miles ? "

" You seem to have heard all about it."

" We didn't hear the beginning. Oh, do tell us."

" It's that fishing friend of his," said Mrs. Kennedy, appearing from the hall with her hands full of cutlery.

She was a small dark woman who always expected the worst, which was a good thing in a family where the worst so often happened. " He wants to come here next week with his family and he'd booked rooms in Melvick with Mrs. Maclean, and of course she's just had a stroke and can't have them."

" Personally, I'd as soon have a stroke as have my friend's wife," said Dr. Kennedy. " She wears a cloak and does water-colours. However, he's a nice fellow, and his daughter will be company for you two."

" Oh," said Sovra, rather taken aback by this.

" Oh," said Ian, in the sort of voice that might mean anything and usually means that you don't like the idea at all.

" Anyway, they've nowhere to go now, and your father wants to have them here," said Mrs. Kennedy, in rather the same tone of voice. " He thinks you might be able to sleep in the bothy, but I doubt very much——"

" Oh do let us ! " cried Sovra. " We'd be perfectly all right. We'd help in the house and you wouldn't have to bother with extra cooking because we could do our own——"

" All right, not so fast," said her mother. " I'll have to consider it. Come and lay the table if you're feeling so helpful. Ian, help your father with his boots. Tea's nearly ready."

Ian sat down on the grass and rubbed a boot with dubbin, his head a little on one side because he was thinking so hard. He was not thinking about the bothy or the probable visitors or even about stone coracles. He was trying to recall something he thought he had seen on the shore of Fionn-ard. By shutting his eyes and screwing up his mind he could see it all as clearly as if he were really looking at it—the cliffs, the waterfall, and the swooping seagulls. There was the gull he was waiting for ; wheeling down and disappearing—yes, disappearing and suddenly flying out again beyond the curving arch of water.

"That's it," he said aloud, and opened his eyes. Fionn-ard's rocks and foam dissolved and swam in mist for a moment, and then he found he was looking at the familiar grass bank and gravel path in front of his home. His father glanced at him in amusement.

"What on earth are you dreaming about ? "

Ian smiled patiently.

"It flew right behind it," he replied, as though that would explain everything.

"Clean daft," said his father, and went in to tea.

2. Burning Down the Bothy

THE WEATHER STAYED
fine during the next few days. Mrs. Kennedy said
that the rain was saving itself up for when the visitors
arrived. Dr. Kennedy began to be worried about not
having enough water in the burns for fishing, and could
be seen stopping his car and leaning out to listen when-
ever he crossed a bridge. Ian and Sovra had a busy
time collecting their things for camping, and going out
in the boat. They explored the nearest islands, but
never ventured as far as Castle Island or Fionn-ard,
though they decided they would go to both places as soon
as their mother was occupied with her visitors.

Dr. Kennedy's fishing friend was called Tom Paget.
His daughter, who was going to be company for Ian and
Sovra, was called Ann and was about Ian's age. Nobody knew anything more about her ; Dr. Kennedy said
that he had never seen her, but he had seen her
mother once and heaven forbid that she should take
after her.

" Supposing heaven doesn't forbid ? " asked Ian.
" We won't have to have her around all the time if she's
frightful, will we ? "

" You will be polite to her, whatever she's like," said
Dr. Kennedy sternly.

" At any rate," said Sovra, as they carried their camp-beds out to the bothy that evening, " we can be out here most of the time by ourselves, and we needn't see them at all if we're careful."

" I hope they're very respectable," said Ian. " Then Mother will be glad if we'll keep out of the way. We don't look like respectable people's children."

They looked at each other ; dirty and dishevelled and wearing their oldest clothes, they were not a sight to gladden a mother's heart, especially if that mother was entertaining guests.

The bothy stood at the edge of a wood of oaks and birches, just above the little burn, and hidden from the house by a heathery mound. It was a small wooden hut, built long ago as a shepherd's shelter, and repaired with odd bits of wood by Dr. Kennedy for his children to rough it in. It had no fireplace or chimney, so the fire had to be laid in a sheltered corner between two rocks, just beside the door. Here they had cooked all their meals except dinner during the last few days, practising for the time when they actually went to live there.

" It will be a fine night," said Sovra, looking up at the clear evening sky. The sun was still high, but there was an unmistakable late-afternoon feel in the air, as if the shadows were trying to grow longer without anyone noticing.

" I wish we could sleep right outside. It's very dry," said Ian, rubbing his foot along the brittle grass, so dry indeed that it seemed withered as it grew. " I suppose it'll be dewy, though."

" Well, nobody can call the bothy damp now, anyway.

Come on, let's put up the beds and get the fire lighted. Mind those eggs, we're having them for supper."

The inside of the bothy was rather a mess. There was a wide shelf on one wall, loaded with crockery and tins and pots and pans, which had overflowed onto the floor among shoes and blankets and candles. The eggs nestled trustfully on a pile of mackintoshes, and the butter had somehow found its way into a tin bowl, where it lay looking more like soap than butter has any right to.

" It looks like Robinson Crusoe's hut after his goat went mad in it," said Ian.

" Did it go mad ? "

" I expect so. I don't know. What will we do with these beds ? "

Sovra started trying to clear up the mess, while Ian stood feeling helpless. She piled all the things from one side on the other side and made a clear space, where they put up one camp-bed. Then they piled everything on this while they dealt with the other.

" There," said Sovra, rather breathless, for the end pieces of the beds were difficult to get on.

" We've got to sleep somewhere," said Ian. Both beds were by now heaped with things.

" We'll tidy up later," said Sovra. " You go and light the fire."

The sun was beginning to slant down towards the dim islands when Ian went out again, and the midges were starting to bite. He set about collecting firewood hastily, in order to have the smoke of the fire to keep off the midges when they became really fierce. There were plenty of dead branches in the wood, and smaller twigs down by the burn. When he reached the edge of the water he looked towards the sea, and frowned, for the house could be seen in all its ugliness, and the view of the lonely loch and hills was quite spoilt.

" I wish we could go right away somewhere and be miles from any house or any other people," he thought. The bothy was much too near the house, and the visitors would be bound to come and look at it and make silly remarks about camping out. The girl might even want to join them. Ian shuddered.

However, it was certainly better to camp in the bothy than to have to live in the house, and perhaps they could escape into the woods if they saw anyone coming. Ian went back among the trees, where the house could not be seen, and gathered branches until he had both arms full and no spare hand to beat off the midges. These were coming out now in full force—six o'clock until eight was their time for food and exercise.

" Come on," called Sovra from inside the bothy. " I've got all the supper things, except the dripping. Have you seen it anywhere ?   In a square tin."

" No," said Ian, looking vaguely around him. " Not exactly *seen* it."

" Och, well, it doesn't matter. I'll poach the eggs instead."

" I bet the fire won't burn."

" Surely it will, everything's so dry."

" We're not good at fires," said Ian, arranging some twigs over a bundle of dry grass and dead heather.

" That's not our fault. Some people just aren't. And some people can put a match to a handful of wet twigs in a bog and have a blazing fire in no time.　Come on, light it now."

"Where are the matches?"

"Oh.　Matches . . . Ian, d'you know what?"

"Yes," said Ian resignedly.　"We've got none left. All right, I'll fetch some.　Aren't we stupid?"

He set off at a run, but almost at once Sovra called him back.

"I've found some!　In this box—oh, and here's the dripping too.　Shall I poach or fry?"

"Poach.　I like to see them going all frothy.　And if you spill them we'll have a frothy bothy."

"Och, be quiet.　You're talking at the fire and blowing it out."　Sovra had lit the kindling and the fire was soon blazing away, for everything was drier than you could believe if you knew how wet the West Highlands usually are.

They ate an interesting supper of poached eggs, tinned grapefruit, currant buns and fish paste.　Then they sat and hit sparks out of the fire with bits of twig and tried to summon up the energy to clear up the bothy.　Sovra had left everything piled on the beds ; she had not had time to do more than hunt for the supper things.

They had built up a roaring fire to keep off the midges, and it glowed even brighter as the evening grew darker. The sky was still blue, for real darkness would not come for hours yet, but down among the trees there was a chill shadow.

"Oh well," said Sovra at last, stretching lazily. "We'd better clear up a bit."

They shuffled the cutlery and plates to one side, to be washed up in the morning.

"This dripping," said Ian, picking up the tin and sniffing at it doubtfully, "is ever so slightly not all it should be."

"Bother. It's the hot weather, I suppose. Let's see. Ugh, yes."

She loosened the dripping with a knife, and rashly hurled it into the heart of the fire.

Flames shot up, in clouds of evil-smelling smoke, and a violent spitting and hissing drowned their cries of alarm as they leapt back away from the sudden heat. In a second the fire was a red furnace, and the heap of firewood beside it was alight ; in another second the flames had streamed along on a gust of wind and were breaking like waves against the bothy. The wooden wall was dry and brittle ; it began to smoulder and crackle, and sparks flew off into the withered grass, where they grew into little running shoots of flame.

"My sorrow," said Ian. "You've set the bothy alight."

"Oh, *Ian !* " screamed Sovra, rushing at the burning grass and stamping wildly. "*Do* something ! "

Ian picked up a dead branch and darted into the smoky flames, beating at the bothy wall, but the branch burst into fire in his hand, and he stumbled back singed and blinded with smoke.

"No good," he cried. "Can't save the bothy."

"It's spreading, look at the grass ! "

Ian cast a rapid glance behind the bothy. The circle of charred grass was widening, but it was some distance from the trees, where lay the danger of a real forest fire.

" Stop that a minute," he commanded. " We can get some of our things out if we hurry."

Sovra immediately ran to join him, for when Ian sounded as decided as that he could act very quickly. He was already inside the bothy, which was filled with smoke.

The whole of the front wall was flaming, but the fire had not yet reached the roof, and it was possible to run in through the doorway without actually passing through the flames. Sovra grabbed blindly at the end of one bed, and ran backwards with it into the open, Ian at the other end. They dropped it in safety and raced back. The flames had reached the roof, where they eagerly laid hold on the dried moss and weeds covering the rafters.

" Ian, it's not safe ! " cried Sovra, but he dived in again, and in a few seconds they had the other bed out. Most of their belongings were still piled on the beds, and they abandoned the rest while they ran round to beat out the fire in the grass.

This was almost impossible. The harder they stamped, the more the sparks flew out, starting ten new spurts of flame for each one extinguished.

" I know," gasped Ian, rubbing his streaming eyes. " Get a blanket."

He seized a blanket and ran down to the burn, Sovra following with another. He dipped it in a pool, pressing it down to absorb the water quickly, then picked it up in a dripping bundle and panted back to the burning grass. He flung the wet blanket on the edge of the burnt patch, and rolled on it. There was a subdued hissing, and the fire underneath was vanquished. Sovra did the same with her blanket, flinging herself recklessly down in clouds of smoke and steam. They pulled the blankets along to the next burning patch, and gradually the char-ring ground died into a damp blackness, as the fire-fighters toiled on, growing sootier and wetter and more like scarecrows every minute.

At last the circle was closed ; there was no more danger of the fire spreading to the woods. They sank down exhausted, with the breath coming harsh and hot in their throats, and wiped the tears and ashes from their faces.

Behind them the bothy was thoroughly ablaze, though the tough walls still stood upright, and the roof had not begun to sag. Ian turned to look at it, then gave a sort of groan, and exclaimed,

" My boots ! "

" Stop ! " Sovra cried hoarsely, for he had jumped up and was running towards the bothy, but he took no notice.

The flames were blowing back from the doorway, and inside there was a space full of smoke but free of flame. Ian crawled in a little way, sweeping his arms back and forwards an inch or two from the ground as though he were swimming. He hit something knobbly—a boot. The other was just beyond it. He hurled them back over his shoulder, and felt around to see if he could rescue anything else. There was a roaring heat above him, but the wetness of his clothes protected him from its full force.

Sovra came round and saw his feet sticking out of the doorway. The boots were lying behind him. Why was he still inside? Had he been overcome by the smoke? She took hold of his ankles and pulled desperately.

"Stop it!" cried Ian, trying to wriggle out backwards, and finding that you can't do this when your feet are being lifted and pulled from behind.

A saucepan came bounding out of the dim smoky cavern, followed by a tin plate that hit Sovra on the head. She dropped Ian's feet, and he squirmed out, blacker than ever, with charred holes in his shirt where sparks had fallen on him.

"All I could find," he gasped, flinging the boots still further away. They were an old pair of fishing boots discarded by his father; Ian had rescued them from the dustbin and had them studded with enormous nails; he wore them with three pairs of socks for mountain-climbing and loved them like brothers.

"Come away," said Sovra. "The roof is going to fall any minute."

They retreated, and tried to get their breath again, while the flames roared up higher and higher, until there was a splintering crash and the roof fell in.

"Oh how awful!" said Sovra, although half of her was thrilled by the sight of such a fiery disaster. "Can't we do anything?"

"We might try those blankets. It's dying down a bit now."

They tried the wet blankets, throwing them against the walls of the bothy and pulling them away as soon as the wetness had dried up. After a while the flames grew less, and the walls crumbled into a heap of red-hot ashes.

"We'll have to leave it like that." said Ian. "It won't flame up again now. I don't think any sparks could reach the trees from here."

They sat down and looked at each other. They had been fighting the flames for more than half an hour, but it seemed that only one lurid minute had passed since Sovra threw the dripping on the fire. A moment ago, it seemed, they had been sitting peacefully by their little tame camp-fire, looking forward to sleeping in their romantic woodland hut. And now their woodland hut was a glowing mound of embers, very romantic but no use at all for sleeping in, and they themselves were covered with soot, ashes, grass, mud, scratches, bruises and tears—tears caused mostly by the smoke, though some of Sovra's were due to remorse and pity for the bothy's sad end.

"I'm glad we'd had supper," said Ian. "And what a good thing we'd left all our things on the beds. That just shows it doesn't always pay to be tidy. We've saved most of the stuff; there can't have been much left inside."

Sovra sniffed, and nodded mournfully.

"It was all my fault," she said.

"Well, who'd have thought it'd flare up like that? Anyway, it's no use crying over burnt bothies."

She blinked hard, and said,

"I'm not. Come on, I suppose we'd better go and confess."

They tried to tidy themselves a little, but without much success. Feeling guilty and depressed, they left the scene of desolation and went over the ridge and down to the house.

Their parents were in the sitting room, which looked out on to the loch, so they had seen none of the smoke from the fire. They looked up in surprise as the two children came in, and Mrs. Kennedy gave a cry of horror as she saw the state they were in.

" What *has* happened ? "

" Don't be alarmed," said Ian, realizing the moment he spoke that those were the precise words to alarm one's parents most, " but the bothy's burnt down."

There was a moment's horrified silence, then their mother rushed at them to see if they were whole, feeling wildly all over them in case they had lost a leg or so, while Dr. Kennedy gazed at them without moving, and asked,

" Do you mean to say that you've managed to burn that hut completely ? "

" Yes," said Ian. Sovra sniffed harder than ever behind him. " We've burnt it down and what *are* we going to do ? "

3. *Escape and Discovery*

"OF COURSE, BEING THE sort of people you are," said Dr. Kennedy, " you would wait for the only heat-wave we've ever had to throw dripping on the fire."

They had come up after breakfast the next morning to have a look at the ruins of the bothy. Dr. Kennedy had been up the night before, to make sure that the fire was really out, but he had waited until the morning to hear exactly how it had happened. He said he wanted time to calm down. Ian and Sovra had slept in the dining-room on the camp-beds, as their bedrooms were being made ready for the visitors. They did not feel very calm. Their parents had not made as much fuss as you might expect, but Mrs. Kennedy had soon stopped being thankful that they had not been burnt alive, and had begun to worry over the spark-holes in their clothes and the problem of rooms for the visitors, and Dr. Kennedy made it plain that he thought his children were half-witted.

" Well, after all . . . " said Ian. " I mean, *dripping !* Dripping's what you put on toast, not something that burns things down. Nobody's ever told me not to put dripping on the fire."

37

" The trouble with you, Ian," said his father, " is that you know too many completely useless facts, and too few everyday ones. I will say your idea of using wet blankets was a good one. It probably saved the wood."

" Ian was jolly brave," said Sovra, " even if he does know the wrong sort of things. He crawled right in——"

Her brother nudged her violently, but luckily their father was not listening very hard. If he had known about Ian going right into the blazing hut he would never have trusted him out of sight again.

" Well, that's that," he said, turning away. " Now we must decide what to do with you. I'm not going to put off the Pagets. They've got everything settled and the rooms are all ready for them."

" Couldn't we have a tent or something ? " asked Sovra meekly.

" No, you could not. We've not got one, to begin with. It's bound to rain soon, and I don't want you trailing in in the middle of the night and filling the place with damp clothes. No, I'll find you somewhere in Melvick if I can. There may be a room or two not booked up for visitors."

" I wish we could camp out. It would be far less bother," said Ian.

" If you can find some place with a watertight roof and stone walls and a proper fireplace, you can certainly camp out in it," said his father, feeling quite sure that any such place would already be lived in.

" Can we ? "

" Yes, *if* you find anywhere that answers to that description. Now you'd better go and find some harmless amusement. Don't bother your mother, you've caused her enough worry as it is."

They took his advice, and went down to the shore, with enough sandwiches to last them all day. Their mother had told them to be careful and not light any fires and for goodness sake to keep out of her sight until supper-time.

" Och, this is awful," said Sovra with a deep sigh. " I feel like a criminal."

" I don't think they're really angry. After all, we didn't mean to do it, and we saved nearly all our things, and we put it out before it spread to the trees. No, I think it's just that they're worried about the Pagets coming and us having nowhere to sleep."

" Yes. Let's take the boat out, Ian."

" All right. We can't set the loch on fire."

" I hope we won't do anything else silly, though. You know they say things go in threes."

" Agnes always breaks matches," said Ian. Agnes was the girl who came in to help Mrs. Kennedy.

" Does she ? What for ? "

Ian took the matchbox from his pocket, and broke two matches, putting the bits back in the box.

" Burning the bothy was one bad thing, and breaking two matches brings it up to three. So now we can start clear."

" Come on, then. We must get some rollers for the boat some time. The tide's about high now, so it'll be afloat."

" Yes, we must get some rollers. Did you know that
the South Sea Islanders launched their boats over the
bodies of their captives ? "

" Yes, you've told me that dozens of times. You
have got a bloodthirsty mind."

The boat was serenely afloat in the rippled waters of
Camas Ban. Out on the loch a fresh wind was blowing
in from the open sea, and there were streaks of foam
along the backs of the green waves long before they
broke on the shore.

They pulled the boat in until they could wade out to it,
and Ian took the oars while Sovra guided him out into
the loch. In the fresh wind and bright sunshine everything suddenly seemed more cheerful, and they began
to forget about the bothy.

" Where will we go ? " asked Sovra. " The wind's
not much hindrance really, is it ? "

" No. We ought to go out somewhere with the tide,
so as to have it to come home on this evening."

" Out there," said Sovra, waving towards the islands.
There was a blue heat-haze on the surface of the sea,
which made the islands look very far away, but the boat
was moving so smoothly and easily through the water
that nowhere seemed too far to reach in a day. Ian
looked round, and Sovra turned to look at him, both
having exactly the same idea.

" Why not Castle Island ? " said Ian.

" Just what I was thinking. Could we do it ? "

" Och, yes. We've got hours."

" Do you think we'd better ? Breaking the matches
might not really do any good, you know."

" I think we'll be all right as long as we're on the sea,"
said Ian. " All we can do is sink the boat or get
drowned, and it's not rough enough to do either.
Besides, I think the sea likes us."

" I doubt it'll like us all the way, though. The wind's
going round to the north. You can see the waves setting
across the loch already."

" If we keep close to the shore we'll be sheltered,"
said Ian, twisting round again to survey the water ahead
of them. " Come and take an oar for this first bit where
there aren't any rocks. You'll have to guide me when
we reach the point ; the rocks lie out a long way from
the land there. Once we're past that we can go
straight for Castle Island, and the wind will be almost
behind us."

Sovra clambered back from the bows, treading heavily
on Ian and the sandwiches as the boat swayed on the
waves.

" Sorry," she said, taking the oar. " I haven't got
my sea legs yet."

" You've hardly left me any legs at all, you lumpish
loon," said Ian. " I say, there's a gannet on the prowl."

He pointed to the far side of the loch, where a gannet
was flying steadily inland, its long neck stretched out
as it scanned the water below for fish. As the children
watched, it checked its flight and began to swoop round
and down in a narrowing spiral.

" There it goes ! " exclaimed Sovra, as the bird suddenly clapped its wings close and dropped head first
straight into the sea. A spout of water shot up as it
dived, and had hardly subsided when it bobbed up

again a few yards away, swallowing the fish it had caught.

"They say," said Ian thoughtfully, "that gannets have a layer of air between their skins and bodies, which is why they float so high in the water."

"I thought of calling the boat 'Gannet'," said Sovra, "but we don't want it to go diving like that, so perhaps we'd better not."

"'Three times round went our gallant ship,'" Ian sang,

"'And sank to the bottom of the sea.'

"Yes, we don't want it doing that. Donald told me that gannets can only take off against the wind— like aeroplanes—so if you want to catch one you run at it down the wind, and it flies straight into you."

"No thank you," said Sovra. "I wouldn't want to be flown straight into by a bird that size. Are you looking where we're going, by the way?"

"I am now," he replied, hastily glancing over his shoulder. The wind had been gently pushing the boat sideways, and it was much further out than they had intended. Castle Island was now due west of them, and to reach it they would have to row with the wind full on the side of the boat, instead of being able to turn and go with the wind as Ian had planned.

"The wind's norther than ever," said Sovra.

"And the hills are lower, so they're not keeping it off."

"And the current sets across the loch from the north all the time. It's going to be hard work."

They rowed grimly on for a while, and Ian tried to keep the peak of Ben Shian over the viaduct, which meant that they were heading straight for Castle Island. But hard as they rowed, the mountain moved steadily leftwards, and they knew that the island was drifting steadily to north of them.

" My right arm's going to drop off in a minute," said Sovra at last. " It's no good, Ian."

They looked round, breathless with their efforts, and saw the island as far away as ever. The wind was north of north-west by now, and everything seemed to be swept along in its wake ; there were little ripples all over the sea, running with dashes of foam on their backs across the loch towards Fionn-ard. Far beyond the farthest islands, along the faint horizon, fair-weather clouds floated, transparent and round like bubbles. It was as much use to try and reach one of the clouds as Castle Island.

" No, it's done it again," said Ian. " Never mind, we'll get there one day. Where shall we go instead ? "

" We can't go against the wind. It's taking us right across the loch. Shall we go round Fionn-ard and into Loch Drachill ? I've never done that."

" We'd never get back, with this wind blowing. No, let's go and look at the waterfall again," said Ian, suddenly remembering the seagull that had flown behind the water.

They pulled the boat round, and started skimming along with an effortless ease that was pleasant after their hard work.

" I'll row, and you keep a look-out for Dead Man's Reef," said Ian. " And keep a good one, my lass."

" Don't my-lass me in that tone of voice," she retorted, slamming the rowlock into place beside him. " If I thought you were any good as a look-out I'd row myself, but you could have us half-way to Skye and never notice."

Ian smiled kindly and took the oar from her. Sovra knew he was trying to be annoying, so she just made a face at him and went forward into the bows without saying any more.

Soon they came in sight of the reef, just breaking the surface. The ripples surged and foamed round it, and the wind sent up little bursts of spray from them. As they passed the reef at a safe distance they could hear the distant roar of the waterfall, and there it was, as magnificent as ever, plunging from the cliff into the whirlpool.

" Keep pulling out a bit," called Sovra over her shoulder. " We're being sucked in towards the shore."

Ian obeyed, but the current and the tide and the wind were getting mixed up together and doing queer things. Several times the boat slewed round and tried to ram the cliffs, and Ian had to pull right round and head out into open water for a while before daring to go further along the shore.

" We're nearly opposite the waterfall," Sovra shouted through the roaring of the water. She was leaning out gazing anxiously at the heaving surge of waters ahead, dimly seeing the white cataract out of the corner of her eye.

" Rocks ! " she cried suddenly, gripping the prow hard. " Have to go inside them. In a bit—a wee bit more—that's enough. Now straight, as hard as you can ! "

The boat shot along on the edge of the whirling currents, and reached the waterfall and passed it. Ian was keeping so close to the sunken rocks that one oar bumped on their ridges at every stroke.

" Out a bit ! " shouted Sovra, as the boat swayed in the racing current.

" Can't," gasped Ian, struggling with the oars.

They were hemmed in by the sunken reef, so perilously close to the waterfall that the mist of spray drifted over them, cold and clammy. Ian rowed with short jerky strokes, trying to force the boat straight along the shore, while the current battled against him, swirling round in a circle about the foot of the waterfall. The edge of this circle was pressed up into a sharp ridge of water, and the boat hung on this for one breathless moment, balancing between safety and danger.

Ian chose this moment to make a stroke in mid-air, missing the water completely, and collapsed backwards with the oars neatly folded on top of him. Sovra looked round and saw two legs waving helplessly. The boat lurched sideways into the fastest current on the rim of the whirlpool, and for a second or two it was swept round the waterfall towards the cliff. Sovra flung herself forward over the bows again, with a confused idea of fending off the rocks with her fists. The waterfall roared above them, shutting off the sunlight, and the rocks leaned out, sharp and black and fierce with foaming waves, and Sovra felt she must be screaming, though any sound she may have made was drowned by the noise all round.

Suddenly the fierce rocks ahead of the boat seemed to split and fall back, and the boat spun half round and away from the waterfall. Sovra reached out and seized a jutting knob of rock, pulling the nose of the boat out of the current. A dark cave opened before her, and the boat sped in through calm water and beached itself firmly on a bank of pebbles, dimly seen in the wavering half-light. The force of the current sent the boat in so fast that the bows wedged themselves amongst the loose stones, and it lay there safe and still.

Sovra sat back limply and licked her hand where she had scraped it on the rock. She felt dazed by the suddenness of everything. A minute ago they had been out in the sunshine on the open loch, and now here they were in a cave hidden behind the waterfall, which hung like a curtain across the entrance and shut out nearly all the light. The light that did filter through was a wavering network of reflections and gleams from the waves ; it made everything uncertain and as changeable as the water itself.

Ian pushed the oars off him and struggled up from the bottom of the boat, looking quite calm and saying something that Sovra could not hear. She felt annoyed. Here had she been terrified and yet heroic, pulling the boat into safety, snatching them from a watery death by her prompt action, like Grace Darling—(she was rather vague about what Grace Darling actually did). And there was Ian, comfortably hidden under his own feet, seeing nothing of her bravery or the threatening danger.

" How did we get here ? " he shouted, leaning close to her so that she could hear. The waterfall made a deep, booming, plunging sound that was deepened and echoed by the walls of the cave.

" We were nearly under the waterfall," she shouted back, pausing for breath after every other word. " I pulled us out of the current and we landed up here."

Ian climbed out of the boat, patting her shoulder as he passed.

" Good lass," he cried encouragingly. " It takes a girl like you to baffle whirlpools."

" It takes a dumb dotterel like you to lose the oars just on the edge of a whirlpool," she screamed, as he walked away over the pebbles. He went on into the gloom, and after a moment's hesitation she got out and followed. The boat was secure, and there could be no danger in here, unless there were holes in the ground.

They went some way into the cave across sloping banks of shingle and mounds of seaweed and driftwood, through the dim light that grew clearer as their eyes became accustomed to it. The cave was high and narrow, and water trickled down its smooth sides. Soon the walls closed in and the roof grew lower. It was much darker here, but the back of the cave could just be seen, an unbroken wall of rock.

" That's all," said Sovra, as Ian paused. It was quieter here, and there was no need to shout.

" I suppose so. What a pity."

" Let's go back and think about getting out."

" All right. I'll just go right to the end."

" Why ? There's nothing there."

" You never know," said Ian, and went on. He had not taken more than five paces when he stopped and raised his head sharply.

" What's the matter ? " called Sovra. " Can you see something ? "

" No, I can't see a thing."

" What can you hear, then ? "

" Nor, hear, neither."

" Och, come away, then."

" Come here," he said, still with his head lifted. " If I was a blind man and a deaf man, and you set me here, I'd know there was a way out of this cave."

Sovra went up to him, puzzled, but as soon as she was near him she found out why he had raised his head like that. A warm soft wind was blowing down into the dank air of the cave, a wind that seemed full of the scents of Paradise—the mingled scents of grasses and peat and bracken, and heather full of honey. They could not see where the wind came from, but there it was, stroking their faces and making them breathe slowly so as not to miss anything.

" There must be a crack somewhere," said Ian, moving forward hesitatingly. Sovra sucked a finger and held it up to see where the wind came from.

" It's blowing down from this side," she called, turning to the right. " I can't see a thing."

They felt their way along the right-hand side of the

cave, keeping in the warm stream of air, and suddenly Ian leant on a bit of wall that wasn't there, and fell flat on his face on the pebbles.

"You *are* collapsible today," said Sovra, as he struggled to his feet again.

"Things keep on not being there," complained Ian. "First the sea, and now the cave—I say!"

"What?"

"Come and look."

He was standing in a narrow alcove where the rock receded from the main wall of the cave, and as Sovra stared at him she saw that his face was lit up by a dim greyish gleam from above. She squeezed in beside him and looked up, and there was a wide crack in the rock, dazzling with blue sky and sunlight.

"Oh, Ian, can we get up there?"

"Doesn't it smell wonderful? I suppose it's just ordinary fresh air, but it's so clammy in this cave that you notice the smell of it."

"Out of my way," said Sovra impatiently. "If you're going to stand and talk let me see if there's a way up."

She pushed past him and started feeling the rock for possible footholds.

"You needn't fash yourself," said Ian. "There are steps up; I'm sitting on one."

"What!"

Ian moved aside, and in the light they saw that holes had been hewn in the rock at regular intervals, close enough to make a ladder, right up to the crack of daylight.

" What on earth were those made for ? " exclaimed Sovra. " When did you notice them ? "

" Directly I got up. Somebody must have used this way into Fionn-ard, I suppose. It's a lot closer to Melvick than going right round the point to the landing places on the other side."

" How do you know they came from Melvick ? "

" Anyone coming from anywhere else would land on the other side, in Loch Drachill. Nobody would come over from Lochhead to Loch Fionn."

" But nobody would come in under the waterfall like we did, every time they wanted to land here."

" I've a feeling that if we'd come from the other way we could have kept clear of the whirlpool and slipped in close to the rock. It's worth exploring there."

" I'd rather explore here, just now," said Sovra.

" We'd better make sure the boat isn't floating off again. Anything that can happen to us always does."

" I'm no' so sure of that. We've escaped death by burning and death by drowning, all in two days."

" Ah, but you wait for the third time," said Ian gloomily. " Anyway, I'll have a look at the boat."

He went back into the cold echoing darkness of the cave, and Sovra made herself wait for him to come back before she started to climb up the rock ladder.

" It's all right," said Ian, slipping and sliding as he ran back over the loose pebbles. " It's stuck fast, but there is a ring fixed in the rock, so I tied it up just to make sure. It *must* have been a regular landing place. I wonder who . . . "

"Stop wondering and give me a shove. I can't reach the first hole."

He heaved her up, and she reached up and clung to the steps above her, and climbed up carefully, pushing her feet right into the holes. The rock was damp and slippery with moss but the holes were tilted downwards and it was easy to keep hands and feet securely in them. Ian came close behind her, and soon Sovra had reached the top and was pulling herself out onto grass and heather.

The first thing she saw was a clump of harebells, brilliant blue against the pale sunny blueness of the sky, and feathery grass twined in among them, with the warm wind brushing through their thin stems.

"Oh, Ian, where have we got to?" she cried, scrambling out into a patch of bell-heather. He came out after her and stood up to look round.

"I've not been in this part before," he said. "Nobody can have been here for centuries. The sheep don't come here, and even the deserted village is right on the far side, beyond that ridge."

"What ridge?" Sovra dusted the heather pollen off her face, and saw that they had come out on the inland side of the cliffs, where they sloped down away from the sea. Below them lay a green hollow, hardly big enough to be called a valley, with a clear pool in the midst of it. The banks of the lochan were smooth and green, and on the far side there was a thick wood of young birches, rowans and oaks.

"Did you say centuries, Ian?"

"What d'you mean?"

Sovra pointed silently to the far side of the lochan, and Ian looked and exclaimed in surprise. There was a small stone cottage, half hidden in the trees, with the grassy bank stretching down from its door as smooth as a lawn.

" Well, of course there would be a house," said Ian. " We've come in by its back door. It's empty, I suppose."

" The door's all overgrown, but it doesn't look ruined. Let's go and look."

" It's odd the way you come on things quite without meaning to. If we'd set out to find this we'd never have got near it."

" Come on," called Sovra, jumping down from the heathery mound. She ran recklessly down the steep slope, through rocks and rough grass and heather, until her knees gave way and she collapsed on the edge of the smooth greenness surrounding the lochan. Ian gave a shout and followed even faster, but his legs were stronger, and carried him safely right to the brink of the water, where he flung himself down and scooped up a drink, rather like William the Conqueror taking his mouthful of sand.

" It's full of little fishes," he said, as Sovra joined him. " What a surprise for them to see me."

" Oh, isn't this a lovely place ! You can't even feel the wind down here. Look, there's a burn running through the lochan, and it comes down quite close to the house."

" He must have built it there because of that."

" Who ? "

" Whoever built the shieling, of course. I don't know who, any more than you do."

They went round the lochan, crossing the narrow burn that came sparkling down among tumbled rocks, and approached the little house rather nervously, although it was obviously deserted. Its stone walls were grey, and covered with moss and grass ; it looked so much like the trees and undergrowth that it was not surprising they had not seen it at once from the hill.

Brambles had grown across the door, and nettles sprouted from the one small window. Nobody could have been inside it for years. Sovra tried to look in at the window, but the glass was thick and very dirty, and she could see nothing.

Ian was attacking the brambles with a stick, trying to pull them away from the door.

" It's not locked," he said. " I lifted the latch and it moved a bit, but these brambles are holding it shut. Ow ! "

He paused to pull a few prickles out of his hand, and then made a fresh assault.

" It's just the one bit," said Sovra, watching him from a safe distance as he brandished the stick.

" Och, I can't do it with this."

He threw the stick away, and seized the stem of the bramble with determination.

" Ian, don't ! You'll get thorns in you and have blood-poisoning and die ! " Sovra cried, running to help him. Before she got there, however, he had torn the bramble away, and the doorway was clear.

" I've got thorns in me, but I'll not die," said Ian,

sucking the palm of his hand. " Anyway, I've got the
better of that old bramble."

" You're daft."

" Be quiet. I'm going in."

He lifted the latch again, and pushed. The heavy
timbers creaked and trembled, and slowly moved back
on rusty hinges. There was a smell of dust and peat and
cold air long unstirred, and the entering daylight was
clouded by floating cobwebs. Ian moved forward
cautiously, and bumped into something. Sovra felt her
way to the window, and brushed away the cobwebs
that hung there like curtains. More light entered, the
dust of their entrance subsided, and soon they could see
everything in the house.

There was only one room. One wall was taken up by
a built-in bed made of wood, with a cupboard below.
At the back was a wide fire-place, with the chimney
built out inside the room. The third wall was bare,
and the fourth contained the window and the door.
Ian had bumped into a table, small and solid, and there
were two wooden stools by the fireplace.

The two explorers stared round the room, then at
each other.

" It's uncanny," said Ian, in a low voice. " It's just
right for us, isn't it."

" What do you mean ? "

" It's a lovely house. We could easily get rid of the
dust and cobwebs, and it's not damp. You can feel
that."

" It feel nice, like a haybarn or something. It's the
peat dust that makes it smell so heathery, I suppose."

Ian went to the hearth, and peered up the chimney, getting dust all over him.

" It's all overgrown at the top, but we could clear that."

" It's much better built than most of the houses in Melvick," said Sovra. " I'm sure it wasn't built by the people who built the deserted village you were talking about. Where *is* the deserted village anyway ? "

" Oh, down beside Loch Drachill. I've seen it once from a distance. No, you're right. This must have been built later. Well, what do you say ? "

" Say ? "

" Don't you see what I mean ? Daddy said we had to find a place with stone walls and a watertight roof and a fireplace, before he'd let us camp out. Well, we've found it."

" Ian ! Camp in here ? But they'd never let us."

" And what for no ? "

" Oh, it's too far away, and too difficult to get at."

" It's not very far. It wouldn't take more than half an hour to row here, if we came straight across the loch. As for that whirlpool, I'm pretty sure there's a better way in from the other direction."

Sovra stared at him, feeling a sudden longing to come and live in this inviting little house, which as Ian said seemed just made for them.

" It *is* a lone shieling, isn't it ! " she exclaimed. " You know, the poem about ' the lone shieling on the misty island.' Only it's not an island."

" We might see if we could keep it a secret," said Ian thoughtfully, sitting on one of the stools.

"If we camp out, Mummy will have to know where, or her hair'll turn white and our lives won't be worth living," Sovra declared.

"Yes. Och, well, we'll have to work that out somehow. Just look here, Sovra."

She came over and found him pointing at the hearthstone, where blood had dripped from the scratches on his hand.

"Blood on the hearthstone!" he said, gloating over it. "Doesn't it sound like something out of a ballad?"

"There's something else there, look. Something carved in the stone. Wait till I rub the dust off it."

"What is it? Looks odd to me."

"I don't know."

They gazed at the stone, where Sovra had brushed away the dust. A rough circle was carved there, and in it something that might be a branch or a twig of some leafy plant.

"That's a queer thing to carve on your hearthstone," said Ian. "It's just a bit of heather or something. He must have been hard up for something to do."

"I hoped he might have carved his name, then we'd know if he was likely to come back here. It looks as though he's not been back for a long time, though, doesn't it."

"I'm not worrying about that. Nobody would mind us camping here, I'm quite sure."

"Mummy might."

Ian jumped up without replying to this, and went to the door.

" I've just thought of something," he exclaimed.
" The tide will have turned, and it'll be going out.
Those rocks by the waterfall were only just under water
when we were there. If we wait any longer we won't
be able to get out of the cave, unless we wait till high
tide again."

" Oh, we can't do that ! If we don't arrive home
before midnight there'll be no hope of camping out or
doing anything. What a nuisance."

" I know," said Ian. " We'll row out of the cave
and find a better landing place somewhere further
along, where the cliffs get lower. Then we can come
back here and stay as long as we like."

" That's a good idea," Sovra agreed, getting up from
the hearth-stone and dusting herself. " I'd hate to
leave the place now, just when we've found it."

They shut the door behind them and blinked in the
sudden brightness outside.

" This valley is a very nice shape," said Ian. " It's
like something . . . what is it ? "

" The green bit, d'you mean ? Sort of round, with
a bit sticking out each end. Like a bowl with two
handles."

" Yes, that's it. Like the one Donald's got on his
mantelpiece. It's really a loving-cup ; the sort of
thing two people drink out of at once."

" You can't, possibly."

" You could if you sucked hard enough."

" I bet you couldn't."

" All right, we'll try it some time. Old Donald calls
it a quaich."

They passed the lochan and climbed the heathery slope opposite, never pausing until they reached the top and met the wind and the noise of the sea. Then they suddenly looked at each other in alarm.

" Where's the way down to the cave ? " said Sovra.

" We can't have passed it."

" We must have. It wasn't a very big hole."

They turned back and began to search the hillside, but every patch of heather looked like the one where they had climbed out, and they could not find the right one.

" There were some harebells just at the top," said Sovra.

" The whole place is littered with harebells," said Ian, striding through a clump of them. Sovra followed, and suddenly gave a cry of surprise and alarm. Ian turned, to find that she was visible only from the armpits up. She had flung out her arms to keep her head and shoulders above ground, but the rest of her had apparently been swallowed up.

" My sorrow," said Ian. " You've fallen down the hole."

" Oh Ian, I'd like to wring your neck," she gasped, red in the face with fury and the effort of holding herself up. " Pull me up, you idiot, and stop making stupid remarks. I can't find anything to stand on, I don't know where the steps are, and I'll fall right down—"

Ian stooped and lifted her under the arms before she could finish her sentence, and pulled her out onto the heather.

" We'd better mark the place if we can," he said.

" How ? "

" You needn't sound so cross. I wouldn't have let you fall, you know."

" I wouldn't put it past you," returned Sovra, rubbing her elbows but sounding less cross.

" We'll bring up an oar next time, and prop it up beside the hole. That'll do it. Now we'd better hurry. The tide's going out all this time."

When they reached the boat they found it high and dry on the pebbles in the cave. The waterfall sounded louder than ever, and the air was clammy and cold. They shivered as they pushed the boat down into the water, and climbed into it quickly, eager to go out into the sunlight that gleamed beyond the falling spray.

Ian shouted and pointed to the rocks at the side of the entrance, and Sovra nodded, knowing that he was trying to tell her to keep close to the side. There was no room to row, so Ian used one oar as a punt pole, while Sovra held the other ready in the bows to push the boat away from the whirlpool. The boat moved jerkily forward, rubbing against the rocky wall, and as it reached the entrance to the cave Sovra plunged her oar upright into the water, and swung the bows round to the right. Soon they were out in the sun and the warm air, and safely away from the whirling currents at the foot of the waterfall. The boat was gliding along at the base of the cliff, protected from the whirlpool by a sunken reef.

" Look out," called Sovra. " We're running aground."

There was a grating sound, and the boat shuddered all over and stopped suddenly. Ian and Sovra lost their balance and fell in a confused heap with the oars tangled up in their arms and legs.

The boat rocked violently as they sorted themselves out, and slid back into deeper water.

"What'll we do now?" Sovra exclaimed, looking back at the waterfall.

Ian pulled off his shoes, rolled up the legs of his shorts, and climbed over the side into the water.

"I'll see what happens ahead there," he said. "If it gets deep again soon we might be able to pull the boat across this bit. It would be all right if the tide was higher."

He waded past the bows and climbed onto the rock where the boat had grounded. Here the water was up to his knees, and he could see the pebbles and shells in the crevices of the rock, and his toes moving amongst fronds of seaweed like cold green monsters of the deep. He trod cautiously, for the rock was knobbly with barnacles and painful to bare feet, and it was difficult to judge the depth of the water. For a few yards he waded knee-deep, and then suddenly the sea was up to his thighs, and just beyond his feet there was a dark green gloom, where the rock fell steeply away and the sea was deep again.

"It's all right again here," he called, turning round and making for shallow water.

"I think it would float if I got out," said Sovra, peering down over the bows.

"I hope it will. We couldn't drag it all the way.

The keel wouldn't stand it, and nor would our feet. Mind the barnacles."

" Ow ! " she said, wobbling from one foot to the other in the water. " I thought my feet were hard. I'm going to put my shoes on again."

" If I paddle in mine much more they'll fall to pieces. Hurry up, it's getting shallower all the time."

There was just enough water to float the empty boat, and they managed to pull it across the shallows and into deep water without scraping the bottom very badly. The sea here was calm, for the islands in Loch Fionn broke the force of the wind, and the waves swelled quietly up against the cliffs and subsided without any foam or fury. The current that had carried the boat in to the waterfall seemed to have lost its strength on this side of the whirlpool, or perhaps it curved round towards the middle of the loch again. At any rate, there was no pull on the boat except the slight drag of the waves as they rolled towards the shore. Sovra took the oars and rowed slowly along close to the cliff, while Ian kept a look-out for rocks and a place to land.

" They're getting higher all the time," he said, looking up at the cliffs. " And they're much too steep to climb. We'll just have to go on. There's sure to be some low ground where the bog is."

" I say," said Sovra thoughtfully. " You know, I don't think there is a landing place on this side at all."

" The shore's as low as anything by the railway. There must be somewhere there, if not before."

" But that's right up at the head of the loch."

" Och, it's not very far.   Why d'you think that ? "

" If there was a proper landing place, nobody in their
senses would go in under the waterfall and make steps
in the rock and everything.   It must be the only way in
from this side."

" Oh," said Ian, impressed.   " I believe you're right.
Well, we'll soon see.   There's the marshy ground, just
ahead."

The cliffs receded, and at their foot lay a tangle of
bushes and reeds, growing in mud so wet and treacherous
that nothing, not even a rabbit, could find a foothold.
It was hopeless to try and beach a boat there ; it would
stick fast in the oozy shallows, and there would still be
twenty yards of impassable bog in front of the unclimbable cliffs.

" Carry on," said Ian.   " I don't believe this goes on
all the way."

They left the cliffs behind, and now they had reached
the low ground at the neck of the headland, and could see
the banked-up railway line curving from the viaduct at
the head of the loch into the broken hills about Lochhead.   The bog grew even wetter, and in one place
became a trickle of water flowing into the loch.

" There ! " cried Ian, pointing.   " There are some
rocks by the shore, just past the burn.   Pull in a bit.
We can land there, at any rate."

Sovra twisted round and made an uncertain course
towards the shore, rowing with one oar at a time.   The
boat bumped against the rock, and Ian jumped out and
took hold of the bows.   Sovra shipped the oars and
climbed out beside him.   They tied the boat to a tough

little bush growing behind the rocks and left it floating peacefully in the calm shallow water.

"Do be careful," said Sovra. "Those tufts of grass are all right to tread on, but if you fall in the wet bit you'll sink in no time."

"Yes," said Ian, advancing cautiously. "It is a bit sposhy. What would these little bushes be?"

"Juniper, I think. Or bog-myrtle. I never know which is which."

They balanced on the tufts of coarse grass that rose firm and dry from the bog, and advanced slowly until they reached the little burn. On the farther bank the grass was very long and tangled, and when they had crossed the burn, by jumping on to something that looked like a rock and luckily was, they found themselves waist-deep in a wet jungle.

"Just the place for snakes," said Ian hopefully.

"Shut up," said Sovra, looking round for another rock to stand on.

"Rattlesnakes," said Ian, and stumbled over a dead bush that rattled its twigs under his feet. Sovra leapt backwards onto the rock by the burn, and Ian followed almost as quickly, before he realized what he had trodden on.

"If a rattlesnake bites you," he advised, "put gunpowder on the wound and light it."

"What, blow myself up? No thank you. What will we do now? We can't reach the hill, there's nothing but plain bog beyond this grass. Not even a tuft to stand on. Look, Ian."

Ian looked, and agreed. Everywhere else, the ground

was dry as tinder after the hot weather, but between them and the rocky slopes lay a wet weedy morass, much too deep to wade through.

" Let's go right back and find where the firm ground begins," he said.   " If we work along the edge of the bog we may find a way across.   If there is one."

" There should be, with the village there."

" No.   They may just have used boats.   There are lots of places like that."

They had to go nearly as far as the railway before they reached dry ground.   Here it was all very bare ; no bracken or heather, only the coarse matted grass full of saxifrage and wild strawberries.   They explored along the edge of the bog, where the rushes began and grass-of-parnassus spangled the rushes with its shiny white flowers, but they explored in vain, and reached the shore of Loch Drachill without finding any way across the bog.

" There's the deserted village," said Ian, and pointed to the far side of the little bay they had come to.

The opposite shore was steep and green, and close to the shore there huddled the ruins of a group of cottages.

" How sad," said Sovra.   " But they are much older than our shieling, aren't they ? "

" Oh yes, I should say so.   There's a slipway for boats, look.   That must have been the only way for getting there."

" I suppose so.   I'd love to explore them, but it's too far to swim."

" We might try wading round the bog.   It can't go right out into the sea."

" Quicksands," said Sovra, going white. " I couldn't bear a quicksand, Ian. Please don't go."

" Oh, all right. Well, there is the waterfall way in, anyway. We can go there as soon as the tide's right."

" ' Ye'll tak' the high road, and I'll tak' the low road,' " said Sovra, looking longingly at the ruined cottages. " Only there's not any high road at all."

4. *The Secret Shieling*

"ONE OF THESE DAYS," said Ian, as they brought the boat slowly along the coast towards the waterfall, " the train will cross the viaduct just as we shoot in under here, and somebody will see us."

" Could they, from there ? "

" Oh yes. They'd see us rushing to a watery doom, and they might do something about it. You never know. Some people can't let you rush to a watery doom in peace."

" Don't worry about that now," said Sovra anxiously.

The boat was laden with the final lot of camping things and moved heavily through the water. As it met the outermost circle of disturbed currents round the waterfall, it lurched and swayed and tried to slip sideways, and the two oarsmen had to pull with all their might to keep on their course. By hugging the shore and fending off on the sunken reef, they managed to round the corner and reach the entrance to the cave, without being swept along by the current as they had been the first time. The boat wallowed in and dug its nose into the pebbly beach, and Sovra climbed out with the mooring rope, securing it to the ring that someone had fixed in the rock. Ian heaved the boatload of camping gear out on to the beach ; rolls of bedding, a suitcase full of clothes, fresh milk in a can and bread in a big biscuit tin.

" We do have a lot of luggage," said Sovra, surveying the heap by the boat.

" Well, that's the last lot, anyway. From now on this is our home. I feel awfully pioneer, don't you ? "

" I don't feel nearly as pioneer as Mummy thinks we're going to be. I never thought she'd let us come."

Mrs. Kennedy had had many misgivings about their camping expedition, and had at first demanded to know exactly where they were going to be. Dr. Kennedy satisfied himself that they had really found a rain-proof house with a fireplace, which was not on an island, and told his wife that she need not be so anxious.

" They won't go setting fire to themselves again in a hurry," he pointed out. " And if it's not on an island, they won't be any more likely to drown than if they were here."

" Those two could drown in the Sahara if they really tried," said Mrs. Kennedy. " And how are we to know if they're all right, if they won't tell us where they are going ? "

" It's somewhere over towards Lochhead. Ian told me that much. If you like, we'll tell them to send a message every evening by the post van as it leaves Lochhead. Then if there's anything they want, we can send it back on the van next morning."

" Yes, I suppose that would do," said Mrs. Kennedy doubtfully. " We'd at least know when they'd killed themselves."

" Give them a chance," said their father. " They're not as silly as they sometimes seem."

So she did give them a chance, and they took all their
camping things across to Fionn-ard as quickly and
secretly as possible, in case she changed her mind,
although she was a good sort of mother and knew it
wasn't fair to be too anxious.   In a day or two the house
in the green hollow was ready for them, and as far as they
could tell they were the only people who knew it existed
at all.   It had been difficult to row across without being
seen, but by going up to the head of the loch and then
rowing down very close to the shore of Fionn-ard they
had managed to keep out of sight of the road.   Once or
twice they had had to wait for the tide to rise high enough
for the boat to clear the rocks at the entrance, and at
these times they had explored the shore along from the
viaduct and found the best landing-place on the mainland side of the bog.   They had also looked again for a
way across, but in spite of the unbroken dryness of the
weather the bog remained deep and wet and impassable.
This, of course, meant that they might just as well be on a
real island, but the sea was so calm that it was no more
dangerous going by boat than overland.

The camping things were hauled up the rocky ladder
in a string bag made out of part of an old fishing-net, with
a cord to pull it up by.   Ian and Sovra staggered down
the heathery hill with their arms full, and dumped their
load on the smooth turf by the door of their shieling.

" There.   That's the lot," said Sovra with relief.
" Except the things we've forgotten, and I never bother
about those because we always forget something."

" Don't talk so much," said Ian.   " I want to feel how
far away and cut off we are.   Nobody for miles.   No

houses. Just the lochan and the hills and us. Grand.
I say, I *am* hungry."

" I like the way you tell *me* not to talk so much. Come
on, let's get the stuff inside before we have dinner."

" It's very late," complained Ian, pushing the door
open.

" Well, the tide was late."

" It's going to be awkward, having to fit in with the
tide always. What's in this bag I've just trodden
on ? "

Sovra gave him a pitying look and rescued a mess of
brown paper and tomatoes from the floor.

" Well, I have to tread somewhere, and the whole
floor's covered knee-deep," said Ian, balancing on one
foot.

" Put the blankets on the bed over there," said Sovra,
bustling about.

They had brought one camp-bed, which was placed
along the empty wall on the right of the hearth. On the
left was the built-in bed, made of pine boards, about four
feet wide, with a ridge along the outer edge, and the
cottage walls for head and foot. It looked as if it had
been designed for someone ten feet high and three broad.
The camp-bed mattress and blankets hardly covered
half of it.

" Who's sleeping in this enormous thing ? " inquired
Ian.

" You'd better. You always sprawl over the edge of a
camp bed. It'll be hard, too."

" I thought that was why you didn't want it. I'll
get some heather or something for a mattress. I wish

we knew who came here before.   Look, there's a metal
rod across here."

A thin rod was fixed above the outer edge of the bed,
close to the rafters.

" Must have had a curtain," said Sovra.

" It's almost another room," said Ian, climbing up
into the recess.   " If we feel sick of each other we can
hang a curtain and hide."

They were too hungry to bother about cooking anything for dinner.   There was a good stock of tins in the
cupboard, and they had brought enough bread and cake
and cheese and jam to last for several days.   They
pulled the wooden stools up to the table, opened the door
wide, and looked out at the lochan and the heather
while they ate.

After their meal they explored Fionn-ard, wandering
at leisure in the warm sunshine, up the seaward hills and
along on the highest ground, where they could see the
secret green hollow on one side, and on the other the
cliffs, and the waves at their feet.   Loch Fionn stretched
dim and blue to the sound and the islands, and beyond
it lay the hills, Ben Aidalan to the north, Ben Shian to the
east, and others beyond them whose names they had
never discovered.   Miles and miles of sea and hills lay
before them, and no sign of any living thing, except the
gulls on the rocks below, and a gannet beating up against
the wind.

" I can't even see Donald's house," said Sovra, as they
stood on the highest part of the ridge.   " Ours is hidden
too.   So's the road."

" And the railway, except just the viaduct."

They looked back up the loch, and saw the train from the south appearing out of the trees and crossing the viaduct. The wind carried the sound of it away inland, but from the look of its two labouring engines you could tell it was very full.

" There come the Pagets," said Sovra.

" Of course. I'd forgotten it was today. We've just got away in time. I hope they can't see us."

" Och, no, we're much too far away. Come on. What's down here ? "

She ran down the steep hillside, and then stopped short as the ground fell sheer away in a cliff at least fifty feet high. This was the western tip of the promontory, and it seemed as well guarded as the northern shore by unclimbable rocks. Sovra lay on the edge of the cliff and looked over. She never felt dizzy on high places. Below her was a little bay of white sand, lined with tide-marks of seaweed and driftwood and brilliant shells. As the waves fell and slithered back they left curves of gleaming orange and red and white specks, where the shells had been washed up the smooth sand and stranded among the bubbles and foam.

" The singing sands," said Ian, leaning over the edge beside her. She looked at him with curiosity.

" When you tread in the dry sand up above the tide level, or rub it with your hand, it sings," he explained. " Just a shrill sort of squeaking noise it is. Something to do with the sand being made of powdered shells, I think."

" I didn't know you'd ever been round here."

" Didn't I tell you I'd seen the other side of Fionn-ard ? It was ages ago ; I'd nearly forgotten all about it."

" I haven't been round here, I know that."

" No, I know. It was when there were a lot of people at Kindrachill, and they asked Daddy and me to go too. We came along in a motor-boat and had a picnic here."

" It must have been a long time ago. Kindrachill's been empty for years. Ever since old Colonel Gunn died, and I can hardly remember him at all."

Ian was no longer thinking about Kindrachill, the big house by Lochhead. He had seen something black and shining out at sea, and it was coming nearer. It might be a seal.

" Look, Sovra. What would that be ? "

" There are three of it, whatever it is."

" I thought it was a seal——"

" Porpoises ! " cried Sovra, kneeling up to look.

The black things were near enough to be seen plainly ; three shining curved fish that looped up and down, in and out of the water, all together in perfect timing, moving so smoothly that their heads entered the water with never a splash of foam. In and out they slipped, up and over and down, effortless and sleek and entrancing to watch.

" Do they do that all the time ? " wondered Ian. " I must try swimming like that. It looks lovely."

" You wouldn't look lovely. You're not the right shape. You'd be all bony spine," said Sovra. " Let's bathe, though. There must be some way down to the sea."

They went on, rounding the point and climbing for a little way along the steep coast above Loch Drachill. Soon the rocks became lower and more broken, and they found a way down onto a beach of pebbles and seaweed. Ian threw off his clothes and started trying to be a porpoise, but as soon as he thought how funny he must look he burst out laughing under water and swallowed what felt like half the loch.

" Come out here," called Sovra, as he fought his way to the surface, spluttering and choking. She had swum out to a rock a little way off the shore, and was lying in the sun feeling like a mermaid. She did not look like one ; she was far too skinny and brown and knobbly about the elbows.

They sat on the rock and looked up towards the hills inland. Fionn-ard on this southern side was wild and bare, but by the deserted village the ground sloped gently to the shore, and beyond the bog the woods began. Lochhead itself was almost hidden in the trees, though wisps of smoke from cottage chimneys and boats drawn up on the shore showed that it was there.

" You can see the chimneys of Kindrachill," said Ian, pointing to the woods just north of Lochhead. " Let's go and look at it some time."

" I don't want to go anywhere," said Sovra dreamily. " We've got our own secret house in our own secret hollow with our own secret entrance to it, and I'd like to stay here for ever."

While Ian and Sovra lay on the rock and dabbled their hands in the water, the Paget family was just coming to the end of a hot and sticky journey. Dr. Kennedy had

taken the car to meet them in Melvick, and as the train
came in he looked anxiously along it, wondering if Mrs.
Paget was as awful as he remembered. When he saw
her getting out he shuddered slightly, for she was wearing
not only a cloak but also a huge straw hat, sandals made
of pink rope, and several strings of wooden beads that
clicked as she moved. She recognized him at once and
hurried towards him, holding out her hand when she was
still five yards away.

" *How* nice ! " she cried, several times, and then
turned to her daughter who was following more
slowly.

" And here is dear Annabel," said Mrs. Paget, taking
her hand and leading her forward. Dr. Kennedy
blinked when he saw her orange dress and pink coat, and
found himself saying,

" I thought your name was Ann," instead of something
polite like " how do you do."

" Well, it is really," said Ann, who was fair and had a
nice smile. " But Mother likes making it longer, don't
you, Mother dear ? "

At this point Mr. Paget came up with a porter and a
lot of luggage, and by the time all the Pagets and their
trunks and bags and easels and fishing rods were packed
into Dr. Kennedy's car, he had got to the stage of being
called " dear Dr. Kennedy " by Mrs. Paget, and felt like
calling her anything but dear.

Ann looked out at the hills as they drove to Camas Ban,
and sang " The Road to the Isles " under her breath.
She had never been to Scotland before, and everything
looked more wonderful than her fondest dreams ; the

heather so crimson, the hills so sunny, and the orange seaweed all along beside the shining water.

" Oh, dear Mrs. Kennedy ! " cried Mrs. Paget, as Dr. Kennedy helped her out of the car and introduced her to his wife. " *How* nice of you to have us ! "

Mrs. Kennedy felt like saying, " yes, isn't it," but made a great effort to be welcoming and hopeful about the fine weather lasting.

" Oh, no weather hinders *me*," said Mrs. Paget. " I paint every thing I see—rain, snow, sunshine, twilight and dawn. Don't I, Ann dear ? "

" Yes, Mother dear," said Ann.

" And where are your dear little children ? " Mrs. Paget went on, as they entered the house.

" Oh, they're camping over there," said Mrs. Kennedy, waving vaguely across the loch, and wondering what they would think of being called dear little children.

" Camping ! So refreshingly simple. I love the simple life," said Mrs. Paget, her beads clashing round her as she stepped in a sprightly manner up the stairs.

" I'm afraid it will be a very simple life for you here," said Mrs. Kennedy.

" So much the better. I am going to paint and paint in this delicious country. Every corner of it is crying out to be painted. You must tell me how to reach any beauty-spots there are."

Mrs. Kennedy promised to ask her husband to show Mrs. Paget all the beauty-spots within reach, and Mrs. Paget asked him about it at tea-time, just when the two men were hoping to have a quiet talk about fishing.

" Any romantic spot will do," she exclaimed with an eager smile. " But if there is a ruined castle, or an old bridge, or a waterfall, my joy will be complete."

It seemed to Dr. Kennedy that the sooner her joy was complete, the sooner he would be able to get a word with Tom Paget, so he thought hard, and finally said,

" There are no castles anywhere near here, but there are some nice wee bridges, and there's the deserted village over on Fionn-ard, of course. That's ruined all right, but you can't get very close."

" A deserted village ? But how romantic, and how sad. I must certainly paint that."

" Why is it deserted ? " asked Ann, who had said nothing so far, being used to listening.

" I don't exactly know," said Dr. Kennedy. " There are plenty of them up here, you know. People just drift away to the towns because they can't make a living here, I suppose."

" Oh, but it must have a history. A sad one, no doubt, but one I should like to know," said Mrs. Paget.

" If you really want to know," said Mrs. Kennedy, " the man to ask is old Donald along the road here. He had some cousins who lived there, a long time ago."

This seemed to satisfy Mrs. Paget, and she was soon talking about something else, but Ann went on thinking about the deserted village, and wondering where it was, and where the " dear little children " were camping, and whether she would see them. Her holidays were usually rather dull. When it was fine she went with her mother, who sat and sketched while Ann did nothing, and when it was wet she went with her father, who fished while she found worms for him. Sometimes she played with other children, and sometimes her father would stop fishing and take her for a walk or go bathing with her, but most of the time she was by herself.

Ian and Sovra had spent most of the afternoon in the water, swimming and splashing and coming out to lie in the sun when they felt cold. They couldn't remember having such hot weather during their summer holidays ever before, and were determined to make the most of it. The sea-smoothed rocks were burning hot to their bare skin, and the pebbles slid warmly about as they trod on them. The hills beyond Loch Drachill grew more and more hazy as the evening approached, and smoke from the Lochhead cottage fires mingled with the haziness in a blue cloud.

The green hollow was still full of sunlight when they returned from their exploring, and lay below them like an emerald loving-cup full of golden liquid. They came up from the deserted village, and paused on the top of the ridge to look down at their camping place.

" You can't see the shieling from here," said Sovra.

" You can't see it from anywhere except just over there where the cave is," said Ian, pointing to the hill where they had climbed out of the hole. " We must be careful not to leave things lying about on the grass, in case anybody starts exploring the deserted village and comes up here. I don't want anyone to see where we are."

" It wouldn't really matter if they did," said Sovra in her most practical voice. She liked their secret shieling as much as Ian did, but sometimes she got rather bored by the way he talked about it.

" It might," he said sharply. " We don't know who it belongs to, remember. If it was someone in Lochhead, and they heard we were using it, they might come and send us away."

" Oh. Yes, I suppose they might. Come on."

She ran on down the hill, feeling hungry and sleepy and full of sun, with the nice tang of sea water at the back of her throat.

Ian was even hungrier, so they had tea and supper all in one without bothering to light a fire first.

" When it gets cold again we'll have hot tea and cocoa and things," said Sovra, sprawling in the doorway with her mouth full of cake. " But cold milk's nicer just now, don't you think ? "

" Oh yes. Let's have a fire later, though. Just to make it more like our own house."

Sovra turned and looked into the room. The sun was slanting in through the open door and window, lighting up the bare stone walls and wooden table, and shimmering through the dusty air onto the hearthstone and the peat ash in the fireplace. The table was piled with crockery and food, the open cupboard was overflowing with more food, and the beds were heaped with clothes, but the house looked just as inviting as when they had first seen it, empty and thick with dust.

" If I'd built a shieling like this," said Ian. " I'd hate to have anyone else living in it."

" Mm," said Sovra, looking back at the lochan.

" Of course," said Ian, " we're the right kind of people

to live in it. Tidy, respectable people wouldn't belong here at all. Are you listening ? "

" No," said Sovra. " Let's light the fire."

She got up and stretched herself lazily, and went to the cupboard under the bed. Here, to her surprise, she found she had put everything she needed ; matches, paper, and some dry sticks they had collected in the wood. They had brought up some blocks of peat from a stack in the deserted village, and there was a pile of bigger sticks and logs outside the house.

" We haven't forgotten anything ! " she exclaimed.

" Touch wood," said Ian. " That *is* surprising."

Sovra laid the fire in the stone hearth, and lit the paper. The sticks were dry and brittle, and the flames seized on them eagerly. For a moment there was a beautiful blaze, and the whole house seemed to wake up and live, but suddenly a cloud of smoke puffed out, and nearly put out the fire altogether.

" Why did you say we'd remembered everything ? " said Ian resignedly, beating out the fire with a log. " We never cleared the chimney."

" Well, you *are* a two-toed sloth," said Sovra. " I thought you'd done that ages ago."

He raked the peat ash over the glowing sticks, and pressed it down firmly.

" Never mind," he said. " It's not cold and we can get the chimney done tomorrow. We'll have our fire tomorrow evening."

It was still light when they went to bed, and the higher hills were golden in the sunset, but down in the hollow it grew dark suddenly as the sun sank, and the noise of the

burn seemed to grow louder as the light faded. Ian lay
on his enormous hard shelf, and heard a curlew far away
on the hill, calling with a plaintive bubbling cry. He fell
asleep as he listened, still wondering who it was that had
last lain in this bed.

5. A Chase and a Rescue

"DEAR ANNABELLA!" CRIED Mrs. Paget next morning. "How clever of you to find this entrancing path. I feel quite inspired already."

"I found it on the map," said Ann. They had walked along the road towards Lochhead, and turned off down a footpath that led along the northern shore of Loch Drachill. It was a nice path, certainly. It wound and twisted among rocks and heather and clumps of rowan trees, whose berries were just brightening to flame colour. The loch was calm and blue, and the tide was coming in over pebbles and patches of white sand and orange seaweed. Ann looked at the hazy blue islands out to sea, and tried not to hear her mother going into raptures over them. Her father had gone out hopefully to fish in the Fionn burn where it entered Loch Fionn. The burn itself had dwindled to half its normal size, but where it met the salt water there might be a chance of a salmon-trout. Ann thought that when her mother had settled down to her sketching she would go across the intervening ridge and watch her father for a while.

The path curved round the shoulder of a spur of rock that ran down into the loch, and dipped steeply on the far side down to the bay and the bog and the deserted village. Mrs. Paget looked at the little grey houses, lonely in the sun, and the green slope behind them, and said excitedly,

"There it is ! That's my picture. If I can get that done today, it can go to Glasgow to be shown with the rest."

"Oh yes," said Ann in a bored voice. Her mother was always having shows of her pictures, and people often bought a lot of them, but Ann had decided that painting pictures was a stupid business. She had tried to do it herself once and was no good at all, and she hated trying to do anything unless she could do it straight away. She found a comfortable place for her mother to sit, and then sat beside her on a rock and watched the tide coming in.

Ian and Sovra were also watching the tide, on the hill above the waterfall.

"It's not nearly high enough yet," said Ian. "We'd have to carry the boat across the reef, and I'd not do that for all the Pagets that ever Pagetted."

"Och, it must be half-way up," said Sovra. "And it's a spring tide, too. Let's try it, Ian. I want to see what they're like."

"We don't want them to see us. We'll have to lurk about all over the hillside until we find them."

"We could see if there's any message for us first. It might say what they were going to do to-day. Come on, Ian, do ! "

She made for the way down into the cave, looking very decided, and Ian followed her, as he usually did when she said " come on ! " in that tone of voice. They just managed to pull the boat across the shallows beyond the

cave, scraping paint off the boat and skin off their feet—
they had forgotten to put on their shoes, but their feet
were so hardened that nothing hurt them except the
barnacles on the rocks. They rowed slowly along the
shore, looking round now and then to see if there were any
Pagets about, and as they drew level with their landing-
place Sovra exclaimed :

" There's a man fishing, at the mouth of Allt-Fionn.
That must be Mr. Paget."

" There's a sort of pink-and-yellowness sitting up
behind him," said Ian. " I expect that's Ann. Let's
land and hide the boat and track them down."

He pulled the boat round, and they slid smoothly into
the little inlet. There was just room for the bows
between two rocks, and the ground rose steeply on either
side, thick with heather and close-growing broom
bushes, so that from above there was no sign of the
boat at all.

" Let's leave our message first," said Sovra. They
had written a short note for their parents, saying that
they were very well and had got enough food.

" If we keep to the trees they won't see us," said Ian,
looking towards the distant fisherman. They went
quickly through the wood and came to the railway
embankment, where they paused for a moment to pick
some of the wild strawberries that were ripening there.
Beyond the railway ran the road to Lochhead, which
looked like a shadowy tunnel through the trees. Ian
and Sovra turned to the right when they reached it, and
soon arrived at a big iron gate, rusty and overgrown,
between two battered gateposts. Here there was a box

on a post, which had been used as a receptacle for letters
and bread and groceries for the house beyond the gate-
way. Dr. Kennedy had asked the postman to collect
the campers' message from the box every evening as he
came along in his van. Sovra opened the door in the
front of the box, and found a bag of fresh buns and a note
from her father.

" The Pagets have arrived," he wrote. " We want
you to come out with them one day, perhaps to climb
Ben Shian. Mrs. Paget wants Ann to meet you. I
don't know why. She says this country is ' delicious '
and her shoes are made of pink string. Your mother
says don't do anything rash."

Sovra giggled, and gave the note to Ian, who was
staring through the bars of the gate. He read it, and
remarked,

" It'll be rather a frightfulness if we have to be nice to
Ann, if she's like Mrs. Paget. Och well. That's
Kindrachill house up there, you know. You can see
a bit of it, all shuttered up."

" Come on," said Sovra, starting on one of the
buns. " Let's go back now. I've put ' thanks for the
buns ' on our note."

Ian said he had no desire to see any Pagets
before he must, so he went on towards the boat, while
Sovra turned off to see what Mr. Paget and Ann were
doing.

" I'll sunbathe in the heather above the landing
place," called Ian.

" There are four buns left in that bag," said Sovra
sternly.

" All right. I won't eat any more. Don't let them see you."

She reached a thick stretch of bracken and disappeared from sight, crouching down until her head was below the higher fronds. It was hot and green and quiet all around here, but after she had crawled a little way she heard the soft murmur of Allt-Fionn, the burn where Mr. Paget was fishing. She paused to listen, and heard the whirr of the reel as he made a cast. He must be very close. Sovra knelt down and burrowed a little farther, then peered out to find him opposite her on the bank of the burn, intent on the water where his line was drifting. There was nobody with him. Sovra looked all around, but the pink and yellow blob had disappeared.

" I wonder where Ann went to," thought Sovra. " I hope she won't bump into Ian. She'd be sure to want to know where our camping place is."

Ian had put the remaining buns in the boat, so that he would not be tempted to eat them, and was lying in the sun on a prickly patch of heather just above the inlet. The boat itself was out of sight, for the rocks overhung the shore at that point. There was hardly any wind, and the sun moved slowly through the cloudless sky that melted gradually into a sky-coloured sea along the western horizon. Ian lay back sleepily and looked through half-shut eyes at the familiar slopes of the hills, and the craggy range where Ben Shian rose from a wilderness of black scree.

Suddenly he stiffened, and lay very still, for out of the corner of his eye he had noticed a pink and yellow figure crossing the hillside a little way off. It was a girl of about his own age, with fair plaits and a very white skin, wearing a pink shirt and yellow shorts. She walked as if she were bored with everything, until she came to the top of a little mound and looked out to sea. Then she stopped to look at the islands, and stared so earnestly that Ian thought it might be safe to crawl into hiding. He rolled over very slowly, and began to wriggle towards a deeper clump of heather and bracken, but before he had gone two yards he heard her calling,

"Hullo! Who's that?"

He glanced over his shoulder, and saw her running down through the heather. If she went any further in that direction she would see the boat at anchor, and if she decided to watch them rowing away she would find out exactly where they went. . . .

Ian thought fast, and Ann had hardly taken ten steps when he had decided how to prevent her from seeing the boat. He leapt up and started to run away from her and away from the boat, towards the wood and the railway embankment.

"Stop!" she cried after him. "Who are you?"

He took no notice and quickened his pace, for her voice sounded much too near. The ground here was very broken; there were all kinds of hollows among the rocks, some deep and broad enough for a hiding-place. Ian was searching for one of these as he ran, hoping to get far ahead of his pursuer and then vanish. He glanced back again as he leaped from rock to rock, and found that she was catching him up. He could climb and walk in bare feet, but when he ran on rough ground the lack of shoes slowed him down. The rocks were sharp-edged and needed watching, and Ian was looking so hard at the ground under his feet that when it suddenly fell away he was quite unprepared, and ran at full speed over the edge of a ten-foot drop.

Ann had started to run after him out of curiosity, but he ran so fast she felt annoyed and determined to catch him. He looked awkward and thin and leggy, and he had no shoes, and she thought it would be easy, but she had to run faster than she thought she could. She was good at running, even over boulders and heather, and was beginning to overtake him when he suddenly disappeared. She went on with more caution, and came to the edge of the steep rock where Ian had fallen.

He was sitting half turned away from her, with one hand pressed to his forehead.

" Are you all right ? " Ann called anxiously.

" My sorrow," he said, not moving. " There's a stone down here that must be smashed to bits. I gave it a good dunt."

" Oh, have you hurt yourself ? " exclaimed Ann, climbing down into the hollow. " It was stupid to run like that over these rocks."

" It was not stupid," said Ian. He took his hand away from his head and looked at it. The palm was wet with blood, and when Ann came round and saw his face she cried,

" Oh, what have you done ? You're all bleeding."

There was a large bruise on his forehead, already swelling and black, and blood was trickling from a cut below it down into his eyebrows. Ann wished that first aid was one of the things she was good at, and thought at the same time that if she'd banged her head like that she'd probably scream or faint. Ian didn't do either, he just sat and looked vaguely at her.

" You might think," he said, " that a bang like this would be enough to knock me out, but it's not. My head is very hard. Actually, I do feel a bit dazed, and if I sound odd you mustn't be alarmed. I always do talk nonsense, anyway. Where's my handkerchief? Oh, here it is. Good. I'm sure yours wouldn't be big enough, even if you did lend it me and got it all gory."

He pulled his handkerchief from the pocket of his shorts—the only clothes he was wearing—and pressed it against the wound in his head. Ann felt bewildered, and wondered whether he was raving, or whether he was like that all the time.

" Where do you live ? " she asked. " You ought to go home and lie down. I'll help you if you like."

" You're Ann Paget, aren't you ? "

" Yes," said Ann. " Mother calls me Annabel sometimes when she's pleased with me."

" Oh, does she ? Out of the way, Annabel, I'm getting up."

He rose unsteadily to his feet, and looked round for the easiest way out of the hollow. Ann stood ready to prop him up if he fell down again, but to her surprise he began to walk slowly up the grassy slope, still holding the handkerchief to his head. She followed close behind him, and when he stopped halfway up she took his arm and helped him on.

" Good old Antimacassar," said Ian huskily.

" Are you Dr. Kennedy's son ? " she asked.

" Never you mind," he said, wishing she wouldn't ask questions.

He was feeling very queer indeed, but he was still trying not to give anything away. Ann would probably realize who he was, but he hoped he could lead her even further from the boat in the inlet.

" Are you all right ? " she asked again, as they made their way very slowly through the heather. " Ought you to be walking, I mean ? "

" Och, yes. My legs are all right. What did you say you were called ? Animosity or something ? "

" My name's Ann," she said sharply. " Come down and walk along the shore here. My father's up by the stream and I'll ask him to look after you. Can you get as far as that ? "

" I can indeed," said Ian. The boat was behind them now, and there would be no danger in taking Ann along this part of the loch, though Ian was not quite sure how to avoid her father, who would insist on taking him home. If his mother saw him all battered and bleeding, it would be the end of their camping.

" Oh you nice shieling," said Ian to himself, but loud enough for Ann to hear. " I couldn't bear to leave it."

" What are you talking about ? "

" The bed was hard, but I slept all right, and when I woke up, there was the curlew again. It sounded like somebody whistling through a mouthful of water. If I knew what was carved on that stone, I might know who had lived there."

" Wouldn't you like to sit down for a bit ? " said Ann, feeling scared, for none of this made any sense to her.

" No, I'm used to knocking myself about, you know. Sovra—that's my sister—would be very annoyed if she knew what I'd done. She'd call me a witless loon, to go stravaiging about and falling over cliffs. We weren't burnt in the bothy or drowned in the waterf——"

He stopped abruptly, wondering what he had been saying. The sun was blinding on the water and the ground seemed very steep and uneven. Ann's voice sounded far away, though she was still holding his arm.

" Not much further," she said. " It's sand here, too. That'll be easier to walk on."

" Sovra's intelligent, you know," Ian went on. " I know things, but she does them."

The sand felt smooth under his feet, and he began to look anxiously for Mr. Paget, for he knew that the only sandy stretch was close to the mouth of the burn.

" Is your sister really called Sofa ? " asked Ann, trying to get at least one thing clear.

" Sofa ? Och, no. It's Sovra. Mummy likes it. It's the Gaelic for primrose. Sovra herself doesn't like it much."

" Primrose ? How nice," said Ann in a voice like her mother's. " I'd love a name like that. Mine's very dull. How do you spell it, though ? "

" Well, she spells it S-O-V-R-A usually ; it's easier for school. It's really spelt S-O-B-H-R-A-C-H."

" Oh. S-O-B *what* ? "

"Give me that stick," said Ian, pointing to a long twig on the sand. Ann gave it to him, and he began to write in the sand, while she stood back and watched.

SOBHRA, he wrote, and the letters began to run crooked. The C was hardly recognizable, and as Ian finished the H he dropped the twig and fell in a sprawling heap beside the name, and a trickle of blood oozed out along the sand below his face.

Ann stood for a moment in horror. She had often imagined herself as an intrepid nurse on a battlefield, ministering to wounded heroes, but now that one lay at her feet she did not feel at all intrepid and hadn't the least idea how to minister to him. After a second or two she turned from the motionless figure and fled along the shore, calling wildly for her father.

He was nowhere to be seen. She ran up beside the burn as far as the viaduct, but could not find him. He must have gone upstream to look for a deeper pool to fish in. Ann hesitated, wondering whether her mother would be any good, but soon decided that she wouldn't.

"I'll have to go back myself," she said firmly. "And I'll take some water from the stream. People always want water if they've hurt themselves."

It took her nearly ten minutes to find her father's haversack with his lunch and a thermos in it. As she searched the banks for it, she kept seeing Ian's still figure lying face downwards on the sand, with the ripples nearly up to his feet.

"The tide's coming in!" she cried, suddenly

remembering. " He'll be right in the sea if I don't hurry."

Luckily she caught sight of the haversack at that moment, and as soon as she had unscrewed the thermos top and filled it with fresh water she set off along the shore, running as fast as she could. A little spur of rock hid the stretch of sand, and until she had crossed this she did not look up from the water she carried. When she did raise her eyes, however, she stopped and stared in astonishment, for the shore was empty. There was no boy, not a trace of him ; no letters scratched in the sand, no stain of blood, not even any footprints left. The tide had risen and covered the place where they had walked, but the ripples were far too shallow to hide Ian, if he were still lying there.

Ann wondered for a minute whether she had come to the right place. She went along the edge of the water, and came to the faint traces of an S and an O in the sand, dissolving fast under the soft fingers of the sea.

" It *was* here ! " she exclaimed. " And I didn't imagine it all. How on earth did he get away ? He can't have walked far, and he's nowhere on the shore. How very odd."

If she had gone a hundred yards further, and climbed down to the landing place, she would have seen the boat hidden there, with Sovra kneeling in the stern attending to Ian. She had seen him stumbling along the shore with Ann, and as soon as he fell and Ann left him Sovra made a wild dash for the boat, the only means of rescuing him quickly. When she beached it on the shelving sand Ian was sitting up, revived by the waves splashing over his legs. With Sovra's help he reached the boat and subsided onto the floorboards, and she rowed him along to the inlet.

" How on earth did you do it ? " muttered Sovra, dabbing cautiously at the blood on his face. " You might have killed yourself."

" It's not as bad as that," he said feebly. " It hardly hurt at all till just now."

" I saw you jabbering away to that Paget girl. What were you telling her ? "

He looked up at her with a puzzled expression.

" D'you know, I can't remember what I said. I don't think I gave anything away. She must have known who I was."

" You'd written my name in the sand, so you must have been talking about me. You didn't tell her about the house or the waterfall, did you ? "

" I don't think so. I say, do you have to do that ? It's beginning to ache like fury."

" All right, I'll leave it. It needs hot water, anyway. We'd better get home as quick as we can. Ann's probably getting a search party."

" I suppose she'll go and tell Mummy I've bashed my head in, and then there *will* be a fuss," said Ian gloomily.

" Well, we can't stop her. I'll just see if she's anywhere about before I push off."

Ian leaned back and shut his eyes. The blood was beginning to dry in his eyebrows and on his forehead, and felt stiff and hard. It was queer, the way he had hardly felt the bruise at first, and had been able to talk to Ann and walk along the shore, and now he couldn't remember what he had said, and felt so dizzy that the thought of climbing up through the cave made his head spin.

" She's away over to the other side," said Sovra, jumping down from the overhanging rocks. " You sit still, in the middle if you can. We'll soon be home."

She took the oars and pulled the boat out and round close to the shore, rowing as fast as she could. The tide was high enough to float the boat over the shallows, and by keeping right under the cliff Sovra managed to reach the calm water of the cave and escape the whirling currents round the waterfall.

Ian got as far as the rock ladder, and stood looking up at it.

" Come on," cried Sovra sharply. " You've just *got* to get up there. Don't stand dithering. I'll come close behind you."

Ian hesitated, but suddenly remembered that Ann had called him " stupid," in a scornful sort of voice, and it annoyed him so much that he was able to climb out of the cave and down the hill without a pause.

" Lie down," said Sovra, putting a match to the fire. " Good thing we got the chimney clear. I'll make some tea. People seem to cure everything with cups of tea."

" Yes, I'd like some tea," he murmured, lowering his head cautiously onto the hard pillow. " That fire looks nice. Our first fire in our shieling."

By this time Ann had reached her mother, and was

wondering whether she ought to tell her what had happened.

"He *was* badly hurt, really, and he couldn't have gone away by himself. Somebody must have taken him away somehow, and they'll be looking after him. We couldn't do anything unless we knew where he was," said Ann to herself. She looked at her mother, who was so absorbed in her painting that she hardly noticed Ann's presence.

"It's no good telling her," she decided, "She'd probably think I was making it all up, and there's nothing to show I'm not. He *was* a queer boy. I wish I hadn't told him about Mother calling me Annabel. He thought it was silly. That's why he called me Antimacassar, I suppose."

Mrs. Paget laid down her brush and sighed with satisfaction.

"Oh, Mother dear!" said Ann. "Have you finished?"

"Not quite. Come and look, Annabella darling."

"It's awfully good," said Ann, surprised. "What's that smoke doing, though? It's coming from somewhere beyond the hill, not from those cottages."

"Yes, dear, I know. I thought it looked rather fascinating."

Ann looked from the nearly-finished sketch across to the grey houses and green hill, and saw that there was indeed a faint plume of smoke drifting up from behind the hill. It had not been there when Mrs. Paget had started her sketch.

"I wonder if the people who see it in Glasgow will notice that it doesn't belong to the deserted village," thought Ann. " This is a queer place. Smoke coming out of nowhere, and boys coming out of nowhere and then vanishing. I wonder if he's got anything to do with the smoke ? No, I suppose not. But it *is* queer."

6. The Heir of Kindrachill

"WE ARE GETTING ON all right and have lots of food except marmalade. Ian bumped his head on a stone but it's nothing much," wrote Sovra, looking rather guiltily at her brother. He was lying on the wide wooden bed because he felt dizzy if he sat up.

" Are you sure it's getting better ? " she asked.

" Och, yes. It doesn't hurt now, it just feels queer. I'll be all right tomorrow."

" Yesterday you said you'd be all right today."

" And anyway, Ann's sure to tell Mummy about it, and if she's worried there'll be a note telling us to come home, so it doesn't matter what you write. That girl's a nuisance. I thought she would be."

" She must be rather feeble, to leave you lying in the sea like that."

" No, not feeble. She sounded awfully sure of herself. She thought *I* was feeble, all right. She can run quite fast for a girl."

" Oh. She'd think I was feeble too, forgetting the marmalade. Well, I'll take the note now ; the tide will be high enough."

" Can you manage by yourself ? "

" I mayn't be as clever as Ann Paget, but I can row a boat single-handed."

" Double-handed, you mean."

" Don't be so funny," said Sovra. " Give your poor battered brain a rest."

She approached the Kindrachill post-box with a sinking heart, for if her mother wanted Ian to come home it would be the end of their camping expedition. When she read the note that was waiting for her, she felt almost too puzzled to be relieved.

Hope you're all right," it said. " There's a change of weather forecast, so be careful not to catch cold. If your roof leaks, come back and camp in the garage."

Sovra read it through twice, frowning. It could only mean that Ann had said nothing about Ian's accident. Perhaps she hadn't guessed who he was. Perhaps she hadn't realized that he was badly hurt. She had not even told his parents she had met him, apparently. They would have said something about it if she had, Sovra felt sure.

She left her own note, and hurried back to set Ian's mind at rest. There were no Pagets about, for it was early in the afternoon and they were probably just finishing their lunch at Camas Ban.

" It's all right ! " Sovra exclaimed, running in at the open door. " Read this."

Ian propped himself on one elbow and read it with surprise and relief, as she had done.

" Good old Antirrhinum," he said. " I never thought she'd have the sense to keep her mouth shut."

" No, nor did I."

" I've been trying to remember something," said Ian, lying back and putting the note aside. " That carving there, on the hearthstone. I know I've seen something like it before."

" Another carving, do you mean, or real ? "

" A sort of carving. I think it was engraved on silver. Yes, that's it. Something silver that I was taking something out of, not long ago."

" We haven't got anything silver."

" Well, this had a silver bottom, anyway, because I took something . . . "

He paused, frowning under the handkerchiefs that bandaged his head.

" The bung," he said suddenly.

" What ? Ian, are you feeling all right ? "

" Och, don't bother me. The bung for the boat. It was lying on the silver——"

" But Donald had the bung, surely ? "

" That's it ! " He sat up eagerly, holding his head with both hands as though it felt loose. " When I went to fetch it, he told me to get it off the mantelpiece, and there it was, lying in that quaich I was telling you about, and the quaich had a silver bottom, and it was engraved with that branch in a circle, whatever it is."

" Are you sure ? Why would Donald have a thing like that ? "

" I don't know. Unless somebody gave it to him. And if the same person carved it in here, too, then Donald might know about this place."

" No, why ? "

" I'm just working it out. My head's buzzing. Wait

a minute. The person who gave him the quaich must be the one who built this shieling, and Donald might tell us who it was if we asked him nicely."

"And another thing," said Sovra eagerly. "If Donald knew about this place, he might have come here in his boat, and that's why there's an entrance this side of Fionn-ard. It would take you far too long to row right round into Loch Drachill and land there."

"It might just be Donald's own house."

"No. He'd never carve things on his hearth-stone. What would he want another house for, anyway?"

"Let's go and ask him," said Ian, putting his feet over the edge of the bed.

"Not today," Sovra said firmly. "You couldn't row and it's too far for me to row alone. And the tide will be going down now, too."

"All right," he said, feeling rather glad to lie down again. "But if the weather's going to break, we may not be able to see him for days. It's a long way across."

"We'll have to risk that. It may not break just yet, anyway."

In the evening Sovra climbed to the top of the western ridge above the hollow, to see what the sunset looked like. The sky above her was as clear as it had been for days, like deep blue water. There was no wind, and the loch lay still, coloured like turquoise where the sun shone on it, and cold silver in the shadow. Everything looked peaceful and warm, except far out to the west, where a bank of cloud was climbing ominously out of the distance and blotting out the islands. The sun grew red and broad as it sank, and for a short time the hills shone gloriously above the dark glens, but soon the clouds had swallowed up the sun and there was a grey shadow over the world.

Sovra shivered, and went back to bring in more firewood while it was still dry.

The clouds drifted over during the night, and as the wind rose it brought them pressing thicker and lower, and when Sovra and Ian woke up they heard the rain beating against their window and howling round the corners of the house. They put on their thick jerseys, and stayed in by the fire most of the day. The rain lifted a little in the afternoon, and Sovra went out to take the message for their parents and collect the marmalade and some more thick clothes their mother had sent. Ian practised walking up and down the shieling while he was alone, and felt so much better that he ventured out for some more wood.

The rain lasted for three days. Mrs. Paget finished her sketch of the deserted village from memory, and it arrived in Glasgow and was hung up for anyone who liked to look at it. Mr. Paget went out eagerly with his fishing rod, and came in soaked to the skin and very proud of the small trout he was catching. Dr. Kennedy went with him once or twice. Ann got very bored, and spent a lot of time looking at Fionn-ard on her father's map, but could find no house marked on it apart from the deserted village.

On the afternoon of the third day the rain grew thinner, and drifted away to eastward in ragged veils. The western sky brightened, and although the sun was hidden there was enough light in the air to cast shadows and gleam on the wet grass. Towards the evening, when the tide was rising, Ian and Sovra rowed out across the loch, where the waves were quietening after the storm. There was still a black bruise and a scar on Ian's forehead, but he had recovered from the dizziness, and rowed with steady strokes.

" It's rather nice to smell the rain on the grass again, really," he said, as they landed by Donald's house.

" It's rained enough," said Sovra. " I hope it clears up properly for a bit."

" Let's see how Donald's bad leg is feeling. It always knows what's going to happen to the weather."

They found the old man half-asleep by his peat fire, his bad leg stretched stiffly out on a footstool. The daughter who looked after him had gone home to cook her husband's supper, and he was all alone. Sovra knocked at the half open door, and went quietly in, with Ian following her and wishing Donald didn't always treat him like a fool.

They talked politely to the old man for a bit, and then Sovra said,

" Please, Donald, may we look at your quaich ? "

" Aye," he said with a knowing smile. " I thought you had come for something. It's up there."

Sovra took it from the mantelpiece, and they looked at it closely. It was a shallow bowl with two flat handles, made of some transparent yellowish stuff, its bottom covered with silver. On the silver was engraved the mysterious device, a circle enclosing a leafy sprig.

" What is that ? " Ian asked.

" Juniper," said Donald, watching them with curiosity.

" Why ? " said Sovra.

" It is the clan's badge."

" What clan ? "

" The clan Gunn," said Donald.   " What would you be asking for ? "

" Gunn," said Ian thoughtfully.   " I wonder . . . "

" But surely old Colonel Gunn—" Sovra began, but Donald interrupted her.

" I'll not be answering your questions until you answer mine."

" All right," said Ian.   " We want to know about this quaich because we've seen that badge carved somewhere else."   He looked hard at the old man and added, " In another quaich."

" Have you so ? " commented Donald, looking very wide awake and suspicious.   " Another quaich ? "

" Yes, or rather it's a wee glen shaped like a quaich, and the carving's on a—a stone, in the middle of it. Donald, you do know about it, don't you ?   We found it just by accident, and we've not told anyone about it."

There was a pause full of suspense, and then Donald sighed and said,

" Aye, I know about it.   I helped to build that wee house.   How in the world did you two find it by accident ? "

They told him how they had been carried in under the waterfall and had found the steps up from the cave, and how they had kept the house secret from their parents even though they were living in it.   Donald listened with great interest, and told them in return how he had discovered the cave under the waterfall many years ago, and had chipped holes in the rock for a way up, in case he should want a short cut to the village any time. He started to tell them about his cousins who lived in the deserted village long ago before all the people left it, and Ian and Sovra listened patiently as he rambled on, for they knew that once you interrupted his ramblings he would get annoyed and refuse to tell you anything. After Donald had told them about his cousins, he went on to the sad history of the Gunns who had lived in Kindrachill House. They owned all Fionn-ard, and some of the country around Lochhead, but old Colonel Gunn had no children to inherit the house and land, and Kindrachill had been empty since he died.

" There is a story about Kindrachill," said Donald. " When the place is left empty of its heir, they say that he will never return until a fire is kindled on his own hearth there. It was so after the '45. The chieftain had fled to France and the house was bare, and after a while he heard there had been a . . . pardon, is it ? "

" An amnesty ? " said Ian.

" Aye, that will be the word. An amnesty. But he did not know for sure whether he could safely go back home. So he came sailing over from France with his wife and bairns, and when they reached the inner sound he climbed up on the rigging to see farther, and as the ship entered the mouth of Loch Drachill he saw the smoke standing up from his own chimney, and knew that his own people were there making ready for him, and showing that it was safe for him to come."

There was a pause, while the two children saw in their minds the French ship floating on the grey waters, and the chieftain leaning from the rigging, ready to go away again from his home if there were no signal of safety. Ian felt a shudder go down his back as he imagined what the sight of that smoke must have meant to him, and Sovra wondered what his wife thought about it. Then she returned to the present, and asked,

"Who is the heir now, Donald? Didn't Colonel Gunn have any relations at all?"

"He had a nephew," said the old man, frowning at the fire. "Young Alastair."

"Oh, I wish we could light a fire for him!" she exclaimed. "Then he might come back, like the other one."

Donald gave her a peculiar look, and said in a low voice,

"I canna be wishing it, Sovra."

"He's dead, Sovra, don't you remember?" said Ian awkwardly.

"Oh, of course. I'm sorry. I'd forgotten. He was drowned, wasn't he? Somewhere in the Far East?"

"Nobody quite knows, do they," said Ian. "Did you know him well, Donald?"

He nodded, and after a moment said,

"He used to come here often at one time. Always out in my boat he would be, over from here to Fionn-ard. It would have been a good thing for all of us if he had come to Kindrachill."

"What was he like?" asked Ian. "I think I saw him here, but I don't think I ever talked to him. He was a lot older than me."

"He wasna much to look at, but he had the good heart

and the good brain, and if it would bring him back I would take my bad leg to Kindrachill and light him a fire myself."

It was surprising to hear Donald speak so earnestly, and it was sad to think of young Alastair Gunn drowned far away and the old man left to grieve over him.

Ian stood up and put the loving-cup carefully on the mantelpiece again.

" Did he give you this, then ? " he said, stroking it with his finger. " And did he build the house over there and live in it, and carve the juniper branch on the hearth-stone ? "

" Aye," said Donald. " I've not been over there for a year and more. Is the roof still whole, and the door hanging well ? "

" It's as good as it ever was," said Ian.

" We've dusted it and aired it. It looks awfully nice," said Sovra encouragingly.

" I wish we could take you there," said Ian. The sad look in Donald's eyes reminded him of a poem he had read. " Do you know the poem about the ' lone shieling on the misty island ' ? It says ' they in dreams behold the Hebrides.' "

Donald looked up at him and wagged his grey head.

" You tell me that when yourself is past seventy with a bad leg, young Ian. Now go and live in your house. It might as well be yours now. Away now, and dinna drown yourselves."

They thanked him, and went out of the dark warm room into an evening grey and damp with a fine mist.

" He got a bit annoyed just at the end," said Sovra.

" No, he didn't. I think he got upset with talking about Alastair. I didn't realize he was so fond of him. Perhaps I asked too many questions."

" Well, we found out a lot, anyway."

" We did that. Sovra. . . ."

" What is it ? We'll have to hurry, you know. The tide must be turning soon."

" I wonder if it's just the hearth in Kindrachill House ? " Ian went on, as they climbed into the boat and pulled up the anchor.

" If what is ? "

" Where you light the fire. To bring the heir back, I mean."

" Yes, of course. Why ? "

He did not answer until they were out on the dim loch, guiding their way by the darker shapes of the mountains. It was not nearly time for the sun to set, but the thick clouds cast an evening shadow over everything, and all the colours had darkened to a rainy grey. Ian shivered a little in the mist, and replied,

" Alastair Gunn had another hearthstone of his own, where he carved his own crest. We lit a fire on it three days ago."

" Really, Ian," said Sovra briskly. " You're as bad as Donald. Alastair's dead, ages ago."

" Yes, it's silly to think about it," Ian agreed.

" It *is* a shame, though," Sovra went on. " Kindrachill's a nice house, in a lovely place, and it ought to belong to somebody. I hate to think of it empty and deserted like the village."

" It must belong to somebody, I suppose."

"Then they ought to have the sense to come and live in it."

"They may have sense but no money," said Ian. "You'd need money to live in a big house like that."

"There's good land around it," said Sovra. "Colonel Gunn used to grow things and keep cows. No, I think it's a great pity about Alastair. He sounds so nice."

"Yes. I wonder if he dreamed about the Hebrides when he was far away."

"Stop dreaming yourself," said Sovra, setting a faster stroke with her oar. "Alastair's dead and gone, and we can't do anything about it, but we'll be here in the mist all night if you don't wake up and row."

7. *Ann is a Nuisance*

THE MIST HUNG LOW ALL the next day, shifting and weaving in the light wind, so that at one minute you could see nothing beyond the nearest rocks, and the next you were looking down avenues of cloudy air at mountains which might have been a hundred miles away, they were so faint and colourless. The sea was calm, and if you kept the boat close inshore it was easy to find your way along to the landing place from Fionn-ard. Next day the mist was thinning all the time, and puffs of wind came in from the south, bringing clearer air with them. In the evening there was a brightness along the western sky, and through a rift in the clouds appeared streaks of blue and gold.

Ian and Sovra climbed to the top of the seaward ridge after supper, and felt the wind blowing steady and warm against their faces.

"It's turning into a fine-weather mist," said Sovra. "I think it will be clear tomorrow."

"Look at the glen," said Ian, turning to look back at the shieling. "It looks as if somebody'd poured porridge into it."

The mist in the hollow was thick and uneasy like simmering soup, and the chimney of the shieling rose above the surface among the tops of trees whose trunks were submerged. The sound of the burn was deadened, and the lochan was hidden altogether.

" It's awfully uncanny. I don't wonder the people here make up stories about ghosts and second-sight and double-gangers," said Ian.

" What's a double-ganger ? "

" I think it's the wraith of someone who's still alive, so there are two of them."

" I wish you wouldn't talk about ghosts, while this mist's about. You almost make *me* imagine things," said Sovra rather crossly. She knew he was still thinking about Alastair Gunn, and during the last two days he had put her off considerably by standing peering out of the window, as if he expected someone to come to their door.

" If I was dead, I'd want to come back, wouldn't you ? "

" Och, stop it ! Look, the mist's clearing away above us now."

Sovra was right. In the morning she woke to find a clear pale blue beyond the window, and when she opened the door the early sunlight was slanting down from above the shoulder of Ben Shian. The air was soft and almost warm, and suddenly Sovra slipped off her pyjamas and ran down into the lochan. The water made her squeal and splash and splutter, and the noise brought Ian out to join her. They raced each other across and back—three strokes each way—and the minnows had a poor time for ten minutes or so. Then they ran up the green slope, dripping and shivering, and dried so violently that they were exhausted and had to go back to bed to recover.

Later in the morning Ann was also thinking of a bathe, though she was not in such a hurry about it. Her mother had decided to walk into Melvick and see how picturesque it was. Mr. Paget had set off with Dr. Kennedy to fish a lochan some miles inland. So Ann was free to amuse herself, and the only thing that didn't seem boring was a bathe in the loch.

She was still wondering where Ian had vanished, and it was with a vague hope of meeting him again that she went along to the far side of Loch Fionn, to the stretch of white sand beyond the burn. She took off her clothes and put on a very smart red-and-white bathing dress and a red cap. Then she took off her smart blue sandals and laid them by her clothes, and stepped carefully down over the rough rocks to the sand.

The sun was warm, and the hill kept off the wind, and she swam about for some time in the slow waves. The water and the light made wavy patterns on the sand ; it looked like nursery marmalade, pale and runny. When at last she waded out and looked up from the creamy foam, she was surprised to see two figures coming through the trees, talking eagerly to each other and not seeing her at all.

" That must be them," said Ann to herself. " Good. I'll be able to talk to them before they run away. They're coming right down on to the sand."

She stood in the ripples and watched them. It was certainly the boy she had chased, and it was certainly his sister. They were thin and brown like gipsies, and their clothes looked like the ones that hang on bushes round a gipsy camp.

Ann felt superior and well dressed, even in her bathing costume, but she had to admire the way they ran down the steep hill, as graceful as shabby gazelles. She walked up the sand, and they noticed her and stopped short, startled and dismayed.

" Hullo," said Ann quickly. " Is your head all right ? "

Ian felt his forehead absent-mindedly, then smiled and exclaimed,

" My sorrow, it's old Anno Domini."

" My name's Ann," said Ann severely, and turned to Sovra, who was staring at her with fierce blue eyes.

" You're his sister, I suppose ? "

" Yes," said Sovra. " Are you going in or coming out ? We don't want to disturb you."

" Oh, I've had my bathe. I had a glorious swim," said Ann in a voice like her mother's. She took off her bathing cap, and shook down her yellow plaits. " Are you going back to your camp ? "

" Some time," said Ian vaguely.

" What happened to you the other day ? " Ann asked him. " I couldn't think how you got away."

" Sovra came and collected me in the boat."

" Ian," said Sovra warningly.

" Oh, I know you've got a boat," said Ann, beginning to feel cold and annoyed. She picked up her towel, and went on,

" I wish I could see your camp. Where is it ? Is it over on the headland there ? "

" I'm sorry, it's got to be a secret," said Ian. " Only one other person knows about it, and we sort of promised him we'd not tell anyone else."

" Oh, well, it'd be all right if I just followed you, wouldn't it ? "

" That would be as bad as telling you, if we let you follow us," said Sovra, surprised.

" Well, I'm jolly well going to follow you, whether you like it or not," said Ann defiantly.

Sovra and Ian looked at each other, wondering how they could prevent her. She could not follow them once they were in the boat, but she could see where they were going, and if she saw them rowing beyond the bog she would know that their camp *was* on Fionn-ard. Ian shrugged his shoulders helplessly, but Sovra frowned and thought hard. If they could gain five minutes start, they could get beyond a spur of rock where the bog ended, and would be out of sight for the rest of the way to the waterfall. But how were they to gain it ? They could tie Ann to a tree, but there might be nobody about to untie her again, and their parents would be annoyed to have one of their guests tied up for days.

Ann had wrapped her towel round her and stood watching them. Sovra looked at her smooth fair hair, her white arms, and her bare pink feet, and had an idea.

" Come on ! " she cried to Ian, and snatching up Ann's sandals she turned and ran as fast as she could away from the shore.

" Here, come back ! " shouted Ann. " You've pinched my shoes ! Stop it ! "

They did not pause to answer, but made for the top of the ridge.   Sovra ran grimly on, but Ian began to laugh, as he leapt from rock to rock, at the neatness of her idea. They reached the top and Sovra flung the sandals onto a big flat rock where they could easily be seen, then they were out of sight of the shore and making for the anchorage as fast as they could go.

Ann started to pursue them at a good speed, furious and disappointed, but as soon as she left the smooth sand she found that her feet were much too soft to carry her over the sharp rocks and heather stalks.   She had to pick her way, jumping desperately from tuft to tuft of softer grass, but it was no good.   In her shoes she could have reached the top of the ridge in time to see exactly where the two fugitives went, but when she had toiled painfully up to the rock where her sandals lay there was no sign of anyone on the farther slope, and she knew that they had vanished again.

She sat down and put on her sandals, feeling hot with anger, and discovered that she had knocked a lump of skin off one heel.

" I *will* find out where they go," she told herself. " Now they've been so beastly I'll jolly well pay them back.   I'll find out where they keep their boat.   But now I'll have to go home.   Bother ! "

She dressed again, and limped along the shore and up the bank of the burn, going under the high arch of the viaduct and on to the road.   Her heel was painful, and she hobbled slowly along, thinking despondently of the stretch of road between her and Camas Ban.

A noise began faintly in the distance behind her, and

became the sound of a motor-bike approaching from Lochhead. Ann plodded along, well to the side of the road, but instead of passing her the motor-bike drew level and stopped. She looked up in surprise, standing on her good foot, and the rider turned round in the saddle and called in a friendly voice,

" Would you like a lift ? "

She stared at him before replying, and saw that he was a slim fair-haired young man, not much to look at, but with nice grey eyes and a pleasant smile. He wore a shabby suit and carried a pack on his back, and a coat was strapped on the pillion behind him.

" How far are you going ? " he said. His voice had the soft Highland sound to it, like all the Kennedys' voices.

" Just along here," said Ann. " To the next house."

" Dr. Kennedy's house ? " he said, surprised.

" Yes, that's it. It's not very far."

" You aren't his daughter, are you ? "

" Oh no. I'm just staying there."

" I thought you couldn't be. He has got some children, though, hasn't he ? "

" Yes, he has. They're both beasts ! " said Ann, unable to control herself. She found that she had been crying with rage as she limped along, and wiped her eyes hastily, hoping the young man hadn't noticed.

" Cheer up," he said, however. " I'll take you along to Camas Ban, if you don't mind holding on to my pack. I'm sorry the Kennedys have been so unpleasant."

" Oh, that's all right. It's just that I'm so angry," said Ann, sniffing hard. " Was that why you stopped ? "

" Because you were crying, d'you mean ? Oh no. I noticed you were limping a bit, and as I've got a bad foot myself I thought it was up to one cripple to help another."

Ann smiled, feeling better.

" Well, it's awfully kind of you," she said. " Would there be room for me on there, though ? "

" I think so. I'll go slowly, so that you don't fall off. Try it and see."

She clambered onto the pillion seat behind him, holding her bathing things in a bundle under one arm, and took hold of one of the straps that fastened his pack.

" All right ? " he asked over his shoulder. " Give me a shout when you want to get off."

He started the motor-bike, and they set off very loudly and slowly. Ann held on tight and watched the road sliding away under her feet. It was quite a long way to Camas Ban, and she felt very glad of the lift, for the sore place on her heel came just where the edge of her sandal pressed, and it would have been an uncomfortable walk. She wondered where the young man was going. Perhaps he was going camping too. He was very sunburnt, but it was sunburn that had worn off and become a sort of brown paleness, as though he had been ill for a long time. He might have been in an accident, thought Ann, and that was why he had a bad foot.

They turned the corner where the road entered the wood behind Dr. Kennedy's house, and she called out,

" Will you put me down here, please ? I go down this path."

They stopped, and she climbed off the pillion and gathered her bathing things under her arm. The young man asked her in a hesitant sort of way,

" Can you tell me if there's an old man living in the next house along the road ? "

" Old Donald, do you mean ? "

" Yes, that's it. Donald Macdonald," he said, looking pleased and relieved. " Do you know him ? "

" Oh no, I haven't even seen him. I've only heard Dr. Kennedy talking about him."

" I just wanted to know if he was still there. I haven't seen him for years."

" Don't you live here, then ? " asked Ann. He seemed to fit in to the place so well, with his old tweed suit and soft voice, that she had imagined him to be one of the inhabitants—a farmer, perhaps.

He frowned and looked up at the hills.

" No, I don't live here. This is just a short visit." He looked back at her and smiled, adding,

" It would be grand to live here, though, don't you think so ? "

" I think it would be *hectically* drab," said Ann, using some of her school slang. " It's not like a proper sea-side place, with lots of things to do. I'd be bored to death."

" Oh. Yes, I suppose you would. This isn't Torquay. That's what I like about it," he said, and stamped on the starter of the motor-bike.

" Thank you so much for the lift," shouted Ann above the noise.

She watched him starting off and careering danger-

ously round the sheep that always lay in the middle of
the road, then she went down the path that wound
through the wood to Camas Ban. On the way she
passed the charred clearing and the ashy ruins of the
bothy. Dr. Kennedy had told her how his children had
burnt it down by mistake, and as she looked at it she
began to feel superior again. They really *were* rather
silly, to go burning things down and falling over cliffs
every other minute. If she watched carefully she
would find out where they were camping, for people
as silly as that would never be able to keep hidden for
long.

Mrs. Paget was sitting on the grass in front of the house
in a deck-chair, surrounded by guide-books. She
beckoned to Ann as she limped down the heathery slope
towards the house, and called excitedly,

" *Such* an interesting morning, Ann dear. Come and
hear all about it. I've been simply *soaking* myself in
local history ! "

Ann went over and sat on the grass, trying to look
interested.

" That's right," said her mother. " And what has my
little girl been doing with herself ? "

" I've been soaking myself in the local water," said
Ann, but her mother hardly gave her time to speak
before she went on eagerly,

" That dear old man—such a character !—has been
telling me all about the deserted village. So tragic,
Annabel dear. Nobody could make a living there, and
the way over got lost and people were drowned trying to
find it——"

" The way over ? " exclaimed Ann, suddenly becoming very interested indeed. " Over where ? "

" Why, through that horrid swamp. It used to be a proper path, but it sank in the mud and now nobody can find it."

" Did Donald tell you about it ? "

" Ah yes, he had to in the end. He was very secretive about it, you know, but I brought out all my arts of persuasion as soon as I saw that there was a mystery, and the poor old dear couldn't resist me ! He just melted completely and told me all about it."

" Did he say where it was ? "

" Across the swamp, dear, didn't I say so ? "

" Yes, but whereabouts ? "

" Oh, I didn't ask for its precise position ! I was satisfied with hearing it was there. Just think of those poor little cottages so pathetically empty."

She went on talking about the cottages, and Ann looked out across the loch and thought hard. Supposing the Kennedy children had found the way across the bog, and were camping beyond the deserted village ? It could easily have been smoke from their fire that Mrs. Paget had put into her picture. But then, why would Sovra bring the boat to fetch Ian when he had hurt himself? Perhaps just because it was easier to go by boat.

" It's been a very dry summer up here," said Ann to herself. " Even this rain we've just had hasn't made much difference. Dr. Kennedy was saying so when he was talking about going fishing to-day. That path through the bog might have appeared again. I *must* find it ! "

She got up quickly, meaning to go back again and look for it, but unfortunately her mother noticed that she was limping, and forgot about old Donald and started to make a fuss and talk about blood-poisoning. Ann was trying to calm her down when her father and Dr. Kennedy appeared.

" Tom dear," said Mrs. Paget, throwing out her hands with a clashing of beads, " tell this child she must take care of her foot. We don't want to have her laid up, do we ? "

" Be sensible, Ann," said her father, not really listening. He hadn't caught any fish, and was wondering why.

" Let's have a look," said Dr. Kennedy, " You needn't worry, Mrs. Paget. A piece of plaster will take care of that. But I tell you what, Ann. If you feel like climbing a mountain tomorrow, you'd better keep that foot still today and give it a chance to heal over."

" A mountain ? How wizard ! " said Ann. " Which one ? "

" I thought we might do Ben Shian, if it's a fine day. That's the one at the head of the glen there, the big one."

" Might as well get some exercise," said Mr. Paget. " No use fishing until there's more water in the streams."

" Ah, what a wonderful thought it is ! " cried Mrs. Paget. " Climbing one of those superb masses and drinking in the glorious views from the top ! How I envy you men."

" Why don't you come too ? " said Dr. Kennedy, looking at her floppy linen hat and pink sandals, and wondering if even climbing Ben Shian would be enough to stop her talking. She shook her head and sighed.

" No, I must be content to stay behind and dabble with my paints," she said regretfully.

" You know you'd hate it if you came," said her husband shortly, and went off into the house.

" Perhaps I shall go and have another chat with that dear old man," she went on.

" Oh, you've been talking to Donald, have you ? I hope he was polite to you," said Dr. Kennedy.

" He was just charming ! Real old-world Highland courtesy. So refreshing ! "

Dr. Kennedy had to suppress a smile at this, for he knew that Donald's old-world courtesy meant that he was thoroughly sick of you and wanted to get rid of you. Ann, too, wondered whether he had told about the path just to make her mother stop pestering him. She thought about that path most of the afternoon, as she sat and rested her foot.

The evening was clear and warm, and after supper Sorva thought she would do some washing. Ian had no clean handkerchiefs left, for they had all been used as bandages for his head. She took the dirty ones down to the burn, just where it ran out of the lochan, and tried to get them clean by beating them with stones. Ian said that was how savages did it.

" Savages don't have handkerchiefs," she objected, as he came to see how she was getting on.

" Och, I don't mean savages, I mean the sort of people with no soap, like us."

" We should have brought more soap. This is no good at all. I'm just tearing them."

He watched her for a few moments in silence, then said hesitatingly,

" I've been having a sort of thought."

" Don't strain yourself," said Sovra, rubbing hard.

" Oh, it was only a smallish thought. A sort of pang of conscience, really."

She sat back on her heels and looked at him impatiently.

" I wish your conscience wasn't so queer," she said. " It always worries about things that don't matter. You didn't have any conscience about pretending your head wasn't badly hurt, when it was. Oh, Ian, you're not going to tell Mummy and get her all stirred up about it now, when it's all over ? "

" Of course not. Stop havering for a minute."

" Go on, then."

" It's old Anna-Maria," said Ian, sitting down and looking worried.

" Oh, I'd forgotten her."

" We were rather beastly to her, you know."

" We had to be. We told Donald we'd keep this place secret, after all."

" Yes, but we needn't have left her like that."

" Yes we need. What else could we do ? "

" I don't know. But she is our guest, in a sort of way. She's probably bored, and that's why she comes tracking us to see what we're doing. She's a nuisance. I'm not sorry for her, but I know I ought to be and it's giving me a mind-ache."

Sovra threw down the handkerchief she was rubbing, and smacked the water angrily.

" Why do you have to go talking like that ? You've made me feel awful now. I don't want to be sorry for her ! It's going to mess up everything if we've got to be nice to her. Oh Ian, you *are* an egg-eyed sharp ! "

" It's no good calling me fancy names. Let's go and say we're sorry we ran away. The tide's coming in, and we can get across and back before the sun goes down."

The sea was calm, and they rowed quickly across to Camas Ban. They went up to the house by the back way, and found their mother in the kitchen hanging socks to dry on the rack.

" Hullo," said Sovra, hoping she wouldn't notice the scar on Ian's forehead.

" Sovra ! " cried her mother. " I *am* glad to see you. Are you all right ? Have you got enough to eat ? Are you sure your beds aren't getting damp ? Did you have enough blankets for those wet nights ? *Ian* ! What have you done to yourself ? "

" Keep calm," said Ian, as she seized him and peered anxiously at his head. " I did that long ago. Sovra told you, didn't she ? We've got lots of food and clothes and dryness and——"

" You never said it was as bad as this," said Mrs. Kennedy reproachfully.

At this moment Mrs. Paget came in, saying something in a sprightly voice, and when she saw Ian and Sovra she clapped her hands and cried:

" Why, how delightful ! Are these your dear little children ? "

" These are Ian and Sovra," said their mother, quite unable to say yes to their being dear and little. They smiled politely but stiffly at Mrs. Paget, who had darted towards them as if she meant to kiss them. When she saw how brown and thin and shabby they were, and how suspiciously they looked at her, she changed her mind and shook hands instead.

" I *do* so want you to meet my darling Annabel," she said. " Why don't we all go in and have a nice comfy family party all together ? "

They looked imploringly at their mother, but she had turned away and was trying to make a noise that would sound like a cough and not like a laugh being suppressed.

Ian had begun to feel really sorry for Ann, instead of feeling guilty about her, so he came forward and said,

" We'd like to see her very much."

" Oh, you poor boy ! " she exclaimed, as he moved out of the shadow where he had been standing. " Mrs. Kennedy, have you seen what your little boy has done to himself ? "

" Yes, I have. It's nothing to worry about," said Mrs. Kennedy. Ian looked at her and grinned. " He did it days ago."

" Oh, but it's a terrible sight ! That must have been a shocking blow. Just look at that scar, and that bruise. Aren't you fearfully worried by it ? "

" Hullo, what's all the fuss about ? " said a bored voice at the door, and there was Ann, so intent on unfolding a map that she came right in without seeing who was there.   When she did, there was an awkward pause.

Ian saw that Mrs. Paget was drawing breath for a rush of enthusiasm about her dear Annabel, so he said quickly,

" Hullo, Ann.   We wanted to see you.   That's why we have come over so late."

She looked at him uncertainly, and then at Sovra behind him.

" Yes, it is late," said Mrs. Kennedy, wondering why her children had to be so uncouth with other children. She had hoped they'd be pleased to see Ann.   She said briskly,

" Why don't you two come with us tomorrow ? We're all going up Ben Shian, if it's fine.   I think it will rain, but if it doesn't——"

" Ben Shian ? " said Ian eagerly.   " Oh, yes ! "

" What about the tide ? " muttered Sovra.

" Och, we'll manage somehow," he muttered back.

" Sovra, do you want to ? " asked her mother.

" Climb Ben Shian ?   Of course I do."

Mrs. Paget started explaining what she was going to do and how she was going to dabble with her paints in some lowly spot, like the poor weak woman she was, and while she did this Ann spread the map on the kitchen table and studied it intently.

" What's that ? " Sovra asked, coming to look.

" What do you mean ?   This is a map.   It's my father's," said Ann in rather a superior voice.

" I've never seen one like that before."

" Haven't you ?   Good heavens."

" Och, we do maps at school, of course, but they are

all big ones, whole countries, you know. We don't
have any like that."

" Doesn't your father ? "

" No. What would he want one for ? He's lived
here long enough to know where everything is."

" Let's see," said Ian.

" There's Ben Shian," said Ann, who liked telling
people things they didn't know. " Where all this dark
brown is. That means it's high ground. There's the
way up, marked quite plain. Do you see that dotted
line ? That's the path. It leaves the road here, by
this house. That black dot means a house. Then it
goes up the valley here. . . ."

Ian and Sovra glanced at each other. They had
climbed Ben Shian more times than they could remember, and knew at least four ways up it, but they were
trying to be nice to Ann, so they let her go on telling
them about the path on the map.

They were so excited about the expedition, however,
that they hardly listened to her.

Mrs. Kennedy made some cocoa, and after they had
finished it and eaten a lot of cake the party broke up,
for the sun was low and would soon be setting.

" I'll come down with you," said Mrs. Kennedy, as
Ian and Sovra started off towards the loch. When they
were a little way from the house, she went on,

" I didn't want to fuss in front of Mrs. Paget, Ian, but
is that bruise really all right ? "

" Och, yes. I just fell on a rock. You don't fuss,
you know, really. Mrs. Paget does, though. Isn't
she weird ! "

" A bit, perhaps. But she means well, and her paintings are lovely. You should have seen the one that was sent to Glasgow to be shown."

After inquiring again about their food and beds and clothes, she let them go, and they rowed back across the silky sea, under a sky as clear as a good conscience.

Ann had climbed the ridge beyond Camas Ban, and was watching them through field-glasses. She followed the boat right across to the waterfall, but there in the twilight and shadows she lost sight of it altogether.

8. *Four Boots and a Mountain*

"WAKE UP!" SAID IAN early next morning, rolling off the broad bed. "We're going up Ben Shian! Where are my boots?"

Sovra watched him struggling out of his blankets and fumbling in the cupboard under the bed.

"They're in there somewhere," she said. "Have you thought yet how we're going to get back this evening?"

"When's high tide?" Ian was half inside the cupboard and his voice sounded muffled.

"Must be about twelve, I suppose. What's that?"

"One boot," said Ian, shoving something out without looking. "Here's the other."

Sovra stared at him as he crawled out and sat up. He had put the boots side by side, and they were both left feet.

"Ian, don't you see?"

He looked at the boots, rubbed his eyes, looked again, then got up and backed away, with a scared expression on his face.

"This one's yours," said Sovra, getting out of bed. "The other's all mildewed. It must have been here for ages."

She felt about inside the cupboard, and brought out

the other two boots, while Ian watched, looking intently at the two which were not his. They were old and battered, and there was damp mould all over the leather, but they were still quite good boots.

" They must be Alastair's," said Ian at last.

" Or Donald's."

" Too small. Donald's feet are like boats. Besides, he'd not go leaving good boots about the place. No, they're Alastair's. I wish we hadn't found them. What will we do with them ? "

" They're quite good still. Would they fit Daddy ? "

" No ! " said Ian fiercely. " I don't want anyone wearing them. Put them back in there."

" Oh," said Sovra, surprised. " All right. Don't fash yourself, I'll do it."

" Sorry," he said, as she did so. " I have a queer feeling about Alastair, I don't know why."

" You hardly ever saw him when he was here, did you ? I didn't."

" I think he was there when we went to the Singing Sands, but I don't remember him at all. But I do have a queer feeling all the same."

Sovra shook her head and shut the cupboard with a bang, and they started discussing how to reach the mainland and get back again in the evening. The tide would be high about mid-day, and they could set out in the boat, but in the evening the tide would be low and they would not be able to row back into the cave. After a lot of discussion they decided to leave the boat where it was, and swim across from the shore by the deserted village.

The sun was beginning to flood the hollow with warm light when they set out, and the scattered white clouds seemed overflowing with silver radiance that made the sky a deeper blue in between.

" It's a nice day for a bathe, anyway," said Ian as they came down to the empty cottages. " Now then, where's that cord ? "

On the pebbles by the slipway, as far along as they could go before the bog began, they took off their clothes and tied them in a compact bundle with one end of the long cord Ian had brought.

" Do you really think you can throw it far enough ? " said Sovra, shivering and full of doubt at the edge of the water.

" Och, yes. I can throw a lot farther than you, you know."

" All right, but hurry up."

" Boys always can," said Ian, wading in a little way so that he would be nearer the opposite shore. " It's because they have an extra muscle in their elbows or somewhere. Like the fourth finger only having one when all the others have two, only the other way round."

" Oh, go *on* ! I want to see where it lands before I start, and I'm freezing."

Ian took the loose end of cord, and started to swing the bundle round his head, as you swing a hammer before throwing it. Sovra watched anxiously, in case the bundle worked loose and shoes came flying out, but it was securely tied and the cord was strong.

The bundle whizzed round faster and faster, and at last Ian let go, and it shot away towards the far shore,

trailing the cord like a comet's tail. There was a thud
as it landed, but as far as they could see it was clear of
the water. They waded in and swam across the mouth
of the bog, Sovra looking down anxiously in case there
were weeds. It was all clean sand and rocks, however,
and soon they were in shallow water again and had
gained solid ground. Ian reached it first, and went to
pick up the bundle.

"What's the matter?" called Sovra, seeing him
pause. "Oh Ian, it hasn't got wet, has it?"

"Not exactly *not*," said Ian, and lifted their clothes
from the shallow pool where he had thrown them.
Water dripped off in a discouraging way, but it had not
soaked through the outer layer, and Ian's shorts were the
only things that were really wet.

"They'll dry on me," he said cheerfully. "It never
matters being wet half as much as people think. D'you
know, we've not done anything really silly for days
now."

"Touch wood, idiot. Now we're sure to."

Ian waved his shorts up and down to get them dry as
they went along the path towards Lochhead, until the
first houses came in sight. Then he put them on, and
they tried to make themselves respectable, to impress
Mrs. Paget.

Dr. Kennedy and the Pagets were waiting where the
path branched off from the main road. Ann looked
hard at Ian's boots, which were enormous below his
thin knobbly legs, and then returned to the map she was
studying, with a pitying smile. Her mother waved gaily
and said how glad she was that the dear little children

were coming too. She was wearing a long shapeless
garment of pink linen, on which she had printed a
pattern of purple horses and green leaves, and on her
floppy hat was pinned a bunch of rowan berries which
clashed horribly with everything.

Nobody noticed the dampness of Ian's lower half, and
they started up the path at a good pace.

"We always hurry up this bit," Sovra said to Ann,
feeling that she ought to try and talk to her. "It's so
much nicer further up."

"That's quite wrong, you know," said Ann. "The
proper way to climb a mountain is to start at a slow
steady pace and keep it up all the way."

"Oh, we never do things the proper way," said Sovra.

"It's more interesting not," said Ian.

"I don't care if it's proper or not," Sovra went on.
"We'll get to the top all right, anyway."

"You seem awfully excited about it," said Ann.

"Well, aren't you? Have you not been up a hill
before?"

"Of course I have. Dozens, and higher than this.
But I don't get all worked up."

"Not even when you begin to see other hills coming
up beyond the farthest ones, and other islands coming
up over the sea, and everywhere stretching out bigger
and bigger?" said Ian, throwing out his arms.

Ann smiled politely and said nothing, and in a moment
they all had to stop and listen to Mrs. Paget telling them
how she meant to slip away by herself quite unnoticed
and dabble in her beloved paints.

"I've found my view!" she announced, springing

to the top of a grassy mound. " Just look at it, everyone.
Packed with Celtic glamour, every inch of it ! "

" That particular inch is an ants' nest," said her
husband, as she prepared to sit down.

They settled her in an ant-free place, and went on up
the path, which wound up more and more steeply over
the bare hillside. The houses of Lochhead drew down
and hid themselves in the trees, and the sea was left
behind, until Loch Drachill was blue in the distance, and
Loch Fionn was farther and bluer still, and Fionn-ard
between them was a mere wilderness of rocks and trees
and barren ridges.

The two men kept up a steady pace, and Ann followed
close behind them, but Ian and Sovra preferred to
wander from side to side and stop for a rest now and
then, letting the others go on ahead.

" She can climb all right," said Ian, looking after
them. " In spite of those daft shorts."

" She's not so bad. She just thinks she knows more
than we do about everything."

" So she does, about most things. But we know she
does, and we don't mind. That annoys her."

Sovra laughed, and they set off at a run after the
others.

" And you know," said Ian as they ran, " she never
told anyone about me bashing my head. That was
decent of her."

The climb was a steep one, but the path took the
shortest way up, and they managed to put off eating the
sandwiches until they had reached the top. The two
men sat and smoked their pipes after dinner, while the

other three dispersed over the rocky plateau that stretched level and barren around the summit.

" Queer that it looks so jagged from below, and so flat from here," said Sovra, following Ian to a point where they could see the view inland.

Ian did not answer. He was trying to count the ranges of hills that lay in fantastic disorder on every side. Bluer and bluer they loomed, with a haze along the farthest ridges, making them so faint that it seemed nothing could be farther, until you saw beyond them other dim and dimmer ranges, and beyond those the pale sky. Every time he came up here, Ian thought he had counted right last time, and every time he found one more somewhere that he hadn't noticed.

Ann was exploring on the other side of the peak. She took the map and the field-glasses, and found a place where the others could not see her, from which she could look down on the whole of Fionn-ard. She looked through the glasses first of all, studying the bog to see if she could find Donald's path, but she could see nothing but a tangle of bushes and reeds and muddy pools.

" It must be there," she said to herself, trying to focus the glasses better. " There, that's clearer. It would be on this side, near the deserted village. But I can't see it ! "

She put the glasses down impatiently, and looked out to sea at the islands, which were so beautiful that for a while she forgot everything else and just stared at them. Then she glanced down at Fionn-ard again—and there was the path ! An unmistakable line threaded the bog, winding in and out among the bushes. It was no more than a faint line of pale colour, but it must be the path.

"Now why couldn't I see that through the glasses?" she wondered, and tried again. It was no good; with the closer view the path was lost, and she had to look again with the naked eye to be able to track its course and learn exactly where it went. There were landmarks along it; bigger bushes or spurs of rock that would guide you safely, if you knew where the path began.

"I'm sure I can find it now," said Ann jubilantly, and jumped up, eager to go down and try. She went back to the men, and saw Ian and Sovra wandering up in their aimless way.

"Hullo," she said, feeling friendly. "Would you like to look through these?"

Ian took the glasses and peered hopefully through them, then passed them on to Sovra.

"Can't see a thing," he said. "It's all blurred."

"Nor me too," said Sovra.

"Oh, you have to focus them first, of course. I thought you knew that."

"You'd be surprised how many things we don't know," said Ian.

"You shut up," said Sovra, twiddling at the glasses to make them focus. "It's no good, I can't get them right."

"Sometimes you can see things better from far off than you would close to," said Ian, and this startled Ann, because she knew how true it was. You couldn't see the path through the bog until you stood on a mountain top miles away.

"Like when they saw Roman roads from the air," Ian went on, "where nobody'd ever suspected them before. And you know those pictures made of dots, that are only dots close to, and turn into pictures when you go further off?"

"Come on, children," called Dr. Kennedy. "We'd better start down again if we want to be home for tea. You two savages, are you coming to have tea with us? We're expecting you."

"Oh good!" said Sovra eagerly. "I'm not a very good cook, you know, and our meals are a bit tinned."

"Well, it's not easy on a camp-fire with only one saucepan and a frying pan," said Ian.

"You ought to get Ann to come and cook for you," said Mr. Paget. "She can produce the most wonderful concoctions from nothing at all."

There was a very dead silence at this, until Ian said hastily,

"Look at those deer!"

They all looked where he pointed, and saw a little group of red deer below them in a rocky glen. Their colour blended so well with the bracken and rocks that at first only one or two were visible, until the whole group began to move, and then there were more and more appearing on every side. They began to file over a low ridge, fifteen of them altogether.

"How wizard!" exclaimed Ann, who had never seen wild deer before.

"I didn't realize there were deer in these parts," said her father. "Do you go shooting, Kennedy?"

"Oh no. There's not much shooting round us, you

know. Not until you get over by Melvick, to the big houses where the millionaires stay."

" Who does the shooting here belong to ? "

" This is all the Kindrachill estate. There's the house, by Lochhead," said Dr. Kennedy, pointing to the roof and chimneys that could be seen among the trees.

" Does anyone live there ? " Ann asked.

" Not now. The house has been shut up for years."

" What a shame," said Mr. Paget.

" Yes, the house is mortgaged, too," said Dr. Kennedy. " Hullo, isn't that your wife ? "

" Yes. And yours," Mr. Paget replied, and waved to the two figures far below. Mrs. Paget could be seen for miles in her pink dress, but Mrs. Kennedy beside her in brown was as inconspicuous as the red deer. They were coming slowly up the path to meet the climbers, and Ian and Sovra set off at a run to join them.

" They'll break their legs," said Ann, as they hurtled down the slope. " Don't they know how to go downhill, either ? "

" They ought to," said their father. " They've been running down hills—and up them—ever since they could walk."

" So have I, nearly," said Ann quickly, but Dr. Kennedy had turned away and was talking to Mr. Paget.

" Hullo, you two," called Mrs. Kennedy, as the runners approached. " Was it nice on top ? "

" It was wonderful ! " cried Sovra, rather breathless. " Och, Mummy, you ought to have come."

" I will, one day," said her mother, who was too busy

looking after her visitors to have time or energy to climb mountains.

"Dear Annabel," said Mrs. Paget, "how she will have revelled in it all ! She feels beauty so deeply, you know, though in her odd way she won't admit it. Ah, this glorious air ! Don't you feel uplifted by it ? "

She went tripping on up the path before anyone could try to answer her, and greeted Ann with a shrill call that made the others feel uncomfortably sorry for her.

"No wonder she's annoying," said Sovra. "Anyone would be, with a mother like that."

"Hush," said Mrs. Kennedy. "Don't start blaming children's faults on their mothers, or I shall have a poor time."

As they all rode back in the car, Mrs. Paget had an exciting story to tell ; she had nearly been run over. She had gone down to the road, where the doctor had parked the car, and was looking for something she had left there, when round the corner shot a motor-bike, missing her by inches or less.

"But he was *so* sorry, poor young man. He stopped and came back and apologised—real Highland courtesy again !—and was really concerned about it and very ashamed of himself. So of course I just laughed it off, because I was sorry for him too, in my odd way, and I blamed it all on my artistic vagueness. I *was* in the middle of the road, you see——"

"Ian walks in the middle of the road too," said Sovra, as Mrs. Paget's story flowed on. Ian wanted to kick her, but they were all jammed so tight in the back of the car that he had to put out his tongue instead.

Neither of them wondered why Mrs. Paget should be so sorry for the young man on the motor-bike, or why she knew he was a Highlander. Ann could have explained about his bad foot and his soft voice, for she knew it must be the man who had given her a lift, but she said nothing. She hardly ever told her parents about anything that happened to her, because they never seemed interested.

" I heard a motor-bike go by as I was taking the short cut through the woods," said Mrs. Kennedy. " It seemed to be going rather slowly. He must have decided to be more cautious."

They arrived at Camas Ban feeling very hungry and exercised.

" This is the best part of a climb," said Dr. Kennedy, as they all started their high tea."

" Oh no !" said Sovra. " Getting to the top."

" Coming down and looking at the view," said Ann.

" Getting your second wind as you go up," said Ian decidedly. " The first half of the way up you nearly die, and then suddenly it gets easy as anything."

" I shan't feel much like swimming home after this," said Sovra absent-mindedly.

There was an instant of horrible silence all round the table, then Ian, who had just taken a mouthful of tea, exploded it all over his plate with a sound somewhere between a bellow and a sneeze.

Confusion followed, with people mopping the table and the floor and scolding and apologizing and trying not to laugh, and by the time everything had calmed down Sovra's rash remark had been forgotten by everyone except Ann. She puzzled over it in silence, wonder-

ing why they had to swim when they had a boat. Ian
and Sovra avoided each other's eyes, remembering how
proud they had been of not doing anything silly for so
long.

" That *was* awful," said Sovra, as she and Ian walked
back along the road. " Do you think they've really
forgotten it ? "

" I tried to blot it out, but they may remember later
on. Och, well, it won't convey much to them if they do."

" It might to Ann. She's awfully curious about
things."

They turned off along the path that skirted the edge of
Loch Drachill, and soon left the path for a more direct
way along the shore. The tide was still far out, and the
water lay peaceful and shining under the westering sun.
For most of the way they had to walk over pebbles and
rocks, but here and there the pebbles gave way to sand,
white and smooth.

As they crossed the first sandy bay, Sovra suddenly
exclaimed, and clutched Ian's arm. He was gazing
vaguely out to sea and seemed half asleep.

" Look ! " said Sovra, shaking his arm.

" Footprints," said Ian calmly. " You know.
People's feet."

" But they're queer, and they go and don't come back,
and I can't see anyone on ahead there."

" He could easily go back along the path, or over the
grass. The tide's been off this bit for hours, you know."

" Yes, I suppose so. But . . . Ian, do just look.
They *are* queer, somehow."

Ian consented to look at the track they were following.

The footprints came at irregular intervals, one of them deeper than the next, and beside them was a line of round holes.

" It's somebody limping," said Ian at last. " That's the mark of a stick. He must have leant on it every other step ; that's why one foot pressed deeper than the other. It does look queer at first, though, doesn't it."

" I wonder who it was. I don't know of anyone with a limp in Lochhead, or Melvick. Except Donald, of course, and he'd never get as far as this."

" Besides, his feet are like boats, as I've told you before."

" Have you ? Oh yes, when we found Alastair's boots."

" These are about Alastair's size," said Ian, studying the marks again.

" Och, come on and shut up about Alastair."

The tide was as far out as it ever could be, and when they reached the bay by the deserted village they found that the bog ended only a few yards out to sea, and they could wade round it shoulder-high, carrying their clothes with them.

" That's one way across, anyhow," said Ian, as they reached the other side.

" Nobody else has been here," said Sovra, looking at the sand that stretched down to the water below the pebbles.

" A man with a limp wouldn't go wading or swimming, if he's the one you're looking for. Come on, let's go home and light a fire."

The shieling looked as secret and inviting as ever when

they reached the hollow, but Sovra was still on the watch
for queer things, and as they came up to the door she
said,

"Ian, did we leave the door shut?"

"Yes. No. I don't know. Does it matter?"

"I don't think we did. But it's shut now."

"I expect it swung shut."

"It's latched, too."

"Now look here," said Ian firmly. "You tick *me*
off all right for imagining things, but what about you?
You know nobody could have been here. Don't you?"

"Yes," said Sovra meekly, and went in without saying
any more, though she looked round very sharply to see
if there were any signs of an intruder. Everything was
as they had left it, however, and Sovra set about lighting
the fire and soon forgot her doubts. It was Ian, after all,
who dreamed of Alastair that night.

9. A Perilous Voyage

"WHAT WERE YOU DOING in the night?" asked Sovra, as they cooked breakfast next morning. "Were you feeling ill? You went wandering round outside for hours."

"I woke up and didn't want to go to sleep again for a bit, so I went out. It was a lovely night."

"It looked lovely, but I couldn't be bothered to get up. My legs are still tired after yesterday."

"It was very clear," Ian went on. "Moon and stars and a light over in Lochhead——"

"You can't see Lochhead from here."

"You can see lights for miles when it's dark. Don't interrupt. I was getting poetic."

"Well, don't. You're not frying the eggs properly."

"Och, I've broken both yolks. I say, we *are* bad cooks, aren't we?"

"Yes, but we don't want Ann to come and cook for us," said Sovra, remembering what Mr. Paget had said about her cooking.

"The owls were raising the echoes," said Ian, busy with the frying pan. "Talking of echoes, did you know that bats find their way about by squeaking and listening to the squeaks bouncing off things?"

" Look out, the kettle's boiling over. *Ian !* "

" Some people can't hear bats," he said, rescuing the kettle.

" Some people can't boil a kettle."

" Shut up, you two-toed sloth. What will we do to-day ? "

" Let's go somewhere nice and do a lot of nothing. The sun's coming out, look."

They waited until the tide was nearly high, and then set out in the boat with a picnic lunch, intending to row across to Eilean Fada and do some fishing. Donald had given them his own fishing lines ; balls of black string with a hen's feather tied to the hook and red wool as a bait. Sovra sat in the stern and unwound one of the lines.

" There probably aren't any over here," said Ian. " Beyond Eilean Fada is where most of the boats go."

" I wish the mackerel would come in. If we do catch anything it'll only be saith, and they're —ooh ! "

There was a jerk at the line, and she coiled it in fast, but all she had caught was a lump of seaweed. She went on catching seaweed, and soon gave up in disgust.

Ian rowed quietly across the rippled water where the light wind was blowing fitfully, first from one side, then from the other. As the boat rounded the end of Eilean Fada, there was a slither and a splash, and they caught a glimpse of a sleek, dark brown body sliding into the water off the sun-warmed rocks.

" Oh, a seal ! " cried Sovra. " I've never seen one so close before."

" There he is," said Ian softly, leaning on the oars.

The round whiskered head had bobbed up twenty yards away, and was regarding them calmly.

" Let's sing to it," said Sovra.

" No, don't. You'd scare it, poor thing."

" Seals *like* singing."

" Not your kind of singing," Ian retorted, but at this point the boat banged violently against the island, and by the time they had fallen over and picked themselves up again the seal had disappeared. They watched for a while, and saw what might have been its head bobbing up again far away, but that was the last of it.

" I wonder if there are any more in the loch," said Sovra.

" Don't expect so. It looked solitary. It was probably a holluschickie," said Ian. He liked queer words like that.

They moored the boat to a knob of rock, and took their sandwiches onto the grass that fledged the higher parts of the long island. The sun was warm, although it had grown cloudier since the day before, and it was pleasant to lie and look at Ben Shian, and know they needn't go climbing it today. Ian grew tired of looking at the hills after a while, and started to read the piece of newspaper the sandwiches had been wrapped in.

" Anything interesting ? " inquired Sovra, flat on her back.

" Advertisements, mostly. Dull. Drear. Oh, here's a chance. Six hundred pounds reward."

" What for ? A seal ? "

" Someone's lost a brooch. Listen to this. ' Lost, somewhere on Knoidart or the Isle of Skye, gold and

emerald dragon brooch.' You'd never find a thing like
that if you hunted for months."

" It must be awfully valuable."

" People who wear things like that in a place like this
deserve to lose them. It must be one of the millionaires
Daddy was talking about. They come here for the
shooting. There are some big houses up beyond
Melvick."

" Well, I'm not going looking for brooches on the
Isle of Skye," said Sovra. "Anything else interesting?"

" The rest's very dull," said Ian, crumpling up the
paper and pushing it back in the haversack. "No
missing heirs or mad bulls escaping, or anything exciting.
Alastair's a sort of missing heir. . . ."

" If you're going to talk about Alastair again I'm
going to row away and leave you here," said Sovra
fiercely.

" All right, don't panic," said Ian, rolling lazily over
and looking at the shore. "I say, there's Mrs. Paget.
She must be doing another picture." He pointed to a
pink blob near the Fionn burn.

" Yes, that's her. You can see that awful pink dress
a mile away. I don't see Ann, though."

" Perhaps she's away by herself. You know, I don't
think she's as bad as she seems."

" What do you mean?"

" Well, she shows off a lot, but I think it's just because
she's bored. I know I'd be, with a mother like that."

" Yes," said Sovra thoughtfully. "And her father's
awfully dull, isn't he. Oh, but she's so *tidy*. Her hair
and everything. That's what puts me off."

" Let's try and untidy her when we get a chance."

" She did like the deer we saw yesterday, though," said Sovra, trying to be fair. " She wasn't bored about them. She sounded quite excited."

" Like she did when you ran off with her shoes ! " said Ian. " I wonder where she is. I wish we could see her. I'm sure she's trying to find out things we don't want found out."

" Perhaps she's cooking a wonderful meal, like her father talked about," said Sovra.

" You cook jolly well yourself," said Ian encouragingly. " And I bet you could beat her at darning socks."

" Any loon can darn socks."

" Talking of sock-darning, by the way, could you mend the collar of my raincoat some time ? The hanger loop has pulled away and it won't stay hung up."

" I will if you'll remind me."

" It's a fiend, that coat," Ian went on. " It lets me hang it up and stays until my back is turned, then down it drops. It did that just as we came out of the shieling this morning, but I was too clever for it ! "

" Oh ; how ? "

" I let it lie, instead of going meekly back and picking it—look, there's the seal ! "

There was the round wet head again peering at them in a friendly way from a distance of about thirty yards. They sat and watched it, fascinated, as it came slowly nearer, but suddenly it vanished, and there was nothing but the dazzle of the sun on the water. Through the warm air came the sound of a distant call, a shrill noise like a seagull shouting " Cooee ! "

" Is that someone calling us ? " said Sovra, startled.

" No, it's not for us. It's Mrs. Paget calling. She must have lost her dear Annabella."

The pink figure was standing on the top of a low ridge, looking this way and that, uttering shrill cries that travelled clearly over the water. Soon she gave it up, and went down to the burn, where she stooped for a moment.

" She wanted Ann to fetch her some clean paint water," exclaimed Sovra. " From two yards away ! Och ! "

" I wish I knew where Ann was. She must have been with Mrs. P. She can't get across the bog, though. I hope she doesn't go swimming across by the deserted village."

" We've got to collect our message yet," Sovra reminded him. " I hope we won't run into her."

They set off again, rowing lazily across the rippled loch, with the shadows of clouds skimming over them as the wind grew stronger. Mrs. Paget was painting the view inland, where the viaduct spanned the burn, and she never turned her head as the boat crossed the loch behind her and reached the hidden inlet. Ian and Sovra went through the wood like shadows, slipping quietly from tree to tree, and looking everywhere for the gleam of a pink or purple Ann, but their caution was wasted. She was nowhere to be seen, and they reached the pillar-box safely.

" Good. More food," said Ian, as Sovra read the note their mother had sent.

" Oh dear," said Sovra. " Listen to this."

She read it out as Ian took out the stores.

"Could you bear to be kind to Ann tomorrow?" Mrs. Kennedy had written. "Mrs. Paget wants to go on a shopping trip and there's nothing for Ann to do. I know she'd love to see more of the countryside than just the bits her mother paints. I told her I would ask you, so will you let us know today? You could take her somewhere in the boat."

"Oh well," said Ian resignedly. "We might try and make her excited."

"I suppose we'd better say yes," said Sovra, starting to write an answer. "Can we manage with the tide?"

"High tide about dinner-time. We could go across about twelve and take sandwiches."

"Mummy says we can go there for tea afterwards," said Sovra, looking at the note again. "How will we get back again?"

"Leave the boat in the landing-place and wade across like we did yesterday, I suppose. It *is* a bore having to think of the tide all the time. We ought to be able to find a way to get across the bog. Floating planks or something."

"Things don't float on mud. They sink. Come on."

They went back with armfuls of tinned food, and made a lot more noise than on their way there.

"Even Mrs. Paget will have heard us," said Sovra. "Let's go down and along the shore."

They slithered down a steep bank onto the rocks, which were piled up in smooth slabs and easy to walk along. As they rounded a corner Sovra exclaimed in a low voice, and trod backwards heavily on Ian's foot, trying to retreat behind the edge of the rock they had just passed. Ian suppressed an indignant cry of " get off my foot ! " and stepped back even more hastily, for there at the edge of the sea was Ann in her bathing dress. Unfortunately he stepped onto a lump of seaweed and his foot slipped, and there was a long and echoing crash as he collapsed with all his tins.

" You *would* do that," said Sovra despairingly.

Ann looked round and saw them, and came running towards them. She was still wearing her sandals and carried her cap in her hand. Five minutes later, she would have been in the sea, and they might have passed unseen.

" You do fall over a lot," she said to Ian, who was trying to collect his load again.

" Well, you're always there when I do fall over," he retorted.

" Sorry," said Ann, looking friendly for a change. " I was afraid you might have hurt yourself again. Have you been to get your mother's note ? "

" Oh yes," said Sovra, remembering what it had said. " Would you like to come out in the boat tomorrow, or is there anything else you'd rather do ? "

" I'd love it," said Ann, going pink and beginning to seem almost excited. " It would be wizard."

" Do you like boats ? " asked Ian.

" Oh, I adore them. When we were in Cornwall last year I used to go sailing."

" Was that wizard ? " he asked.

"Oh yes. Madly wizard. But you don't sail, do you?"

" We do not. I know, Sovra. Let's go to the singing sands."

" All right."

" What on earth are the singing sands ? " asked Ann, wondering whether they were making them up.

" I'll show you when we get there," said Ian. " We'll have to go now. You go and swim."

" All right, don't worry. I won't follow you," said Ann rather crossly, and she pulled off her sandals and held them out to Sovra.

Sovra looked at her seriously, and said,

" We were rather beastly when we ran away from you that time. I'm sorry. We were both sorry afterwards."

" Oh, that's all right," said Ann hurriedly. She gave them a strange glance, and then turned and went back to the edge of the water. The other two watched her put on her bathing cap and dive in off the edge of the rock where the sea was deep. She dived beautifully, and when she came up again she started swimming beautifully out into the loch.

" Now what did she mean by that glint in her eye ? " murmured Ian as they went on along the shore.

" I didn't see any glint. She was just surprised when I said I was sorry."

" No, it wasn't surprise. More as if she knew something we didn't know. Och, well, perhaps we'll find out tomorrow."

They beached the boat in the cave, and climbed up the rock ladder. The hollow lay lonely and peaceful below them, and the sun came out from behind one of the flying clouds and shone on the little lochan.

" Every time we come back it feels as if we'd been here ages," said Sovra, as they entered the shieling.

" Yes, it is a nice house.   Where shall I put these tins ? "

They disposed of the tins, and lit the fire, for the air had a fresh coldness in it from the rising wind.   The firelight flickered over the stone walls and made the house look even more comfortable.   Sovra and Ian lay on the floor and read.   Sovra took weeks over one book ; Ian liked to be in the middle of four or five at once.

Suddenly he gave a queer gasp, and sat up, staring at the door.   Sovra said patiently,

" What is it now ? "

" Sovra," said Ian, turning so white that she sat up in alarm.   " For heaven's sake say you hung up my coat when I wasn't looking."

" Hung up your coat ?   No, of course I didn't.   You mean the one that fell down when we came out this morning . . . "

Her voice died away as she looked where he was looking, for there was his raincoat hanging up on the hook.

" It *did* fall down," said Ian.   " I know it did."

" Somebody must have been here," said Sovra, jumping up energetically.   " What a nuisance !   And I did think we were quite hidden away."

Ian still stared at the coat, and she turned on him angrily.

" I know what you're thinking, you idiot, but even if Alastair's ghost did come back, it wouldn't go hanging up coats. That's the sort of thing no man would ever do. Much more likely to be someone like Ann."

" Ann ! " said Ian, his face lighting up. " I bet it's her. That would explain that look of hers."

" How could she get here, though ? There's no other boat she could get hold of, even in Lochhead."

" No. She must have swum over to the deserted village. She swims jolly well."

" She didn't, though," said Sovra, puzzled. " Her bathing dress and cap were dry when we saw her. They couldn't have dried so quickly if she'd used them already to-day. I'm sure she's the one, all the same. She's tidy-minded, and if she saw a coat on the floor she'd hang it up without realizing what she was doing."

" Oh, this is horrible," said Ian restlessly. " I thought we were safely hidden away, and now these queer things keep happening. I wonder if those boots are still here. . . ."

" Don't be silly," said Sovra, going over to the cupboard. " What would Ann want with old boots ? I put them just to the side here. . . ."

There was a pause, as she felt about in the cupboard, then she said in a changed tone,

" What *would* Ann want with old boots ? "

They looked at each other for a moment. Then Ian got up exclaiming,

" Och, I don't care if the boots *have* vanished. Somebody's been here and taken them. It might have been someone from miles away in a motor-boat, or there may be a way across the bog, after all. Let's have tea, anyway."

They piled more wood on the fire, until the blaze lit up every crack and corner, and it grew so hot that they had to move the table right over by the door to have their tea. The firelight was cheering, and in its radiance they managed to forget about their mysterious visitor and the vanishing boots, and went to bed feeling warm and serene.

The wind was bringing up enormous clouds out of the west, and as the sun sank these turned from a steely grey to a purply blue like ink, and the last light glowed beneath them unearthly bright on rock and water, before the darkness muffled everything in a starless gloom. The waves rose under the heels of the wind, and began to beat so loud against the rocks that their noise came even into the sheltered hollow and mingled with the sound of the burn. Ian lay awake for a while, listening and wondering whether they would be able to reach the singing sands next day. Then he fell asleep, but woke later to a clear starry night gleaming beyond the window. The wind had dropped, but the waves were louder than ever on the shore below.

" The sea *will* be exciting tomorrow," Ian thought. " I wonder if that light I saw last night is there again ? "

But before he could decide to go and look, he was fast asleep.

Next day was clear and cool ; there was a soft breeze and the sun was bright. Ian and Sovra set off in the boat as soon as the tide was high enough for crossing the shallows, and found that the waves running up Loch Fionn were big enough to lift the boat and swing it up and down, but not too rough for rowing.

" It will be a lot rougher round the point of Fionn-ard," said Sovra, looking out at the open sound.

" Och, we can manage. The waves aren't breaking before they reach the shore. We shall have them behind us coming back, too."

At Camas Ban they collected Ann, who had put on a bright green mackintosh over her pink blouse and yellow shorts, in case the spray should wet her. The two oars-men looked very shabby beside her, in their old faded shirts and khaki shorts, but their clothes were so com-fortable and used to getting wet that they had no desire to wear anything better. They wanted to ask Ann if she had been to the shieling, if she seemed in a friendly mood, but they soon discovered that she was feeling superior again, so they said nothing about it.

" This is a clumsy old boat, isn't it ? " were her first words as they started off. She was sitting in the stern while the other two rowed with one oar each. " You ought to see the yachts down in Cornwall. They're beauties. The one I went sailing in——"

" Of course this is clumsy," said Sovra, pulling away energetically. " If it was thin like a yacht the waves would upset it."

" Oh, I suppose they would. All the same, you know, sailing is marvellous. If you go with somebody who knows how to handle a boat, that is. Everyone told me I'd be scared stiff, but of course I wasn't. Where is this place we're going to, by the way ? "

" Out there," said Sovra, nodding over her shoulder. " It's going to be rough."

" Why, this isn't rough," said Ann, looking scornfully

at the waves in the loch. " You should see the real
Atlantic breakers."

The others said nothing. They were beginning to
wish they had never agreed to take Ann out, although
Ian had a suspicion that she might not be as brave as she
sounded when they met the full force of the sea.

They had gone some way down the loch, and were
striking out towards the shore of Fionn-ard, when Sovra
looked round to measure the direction, and saw a
commotion on the surface of the water.   The sea looked
as if it was boiling and bubbling, with a splashing and
scattering and seething, and above all the hubbub the
gulls were gathering, flying round and swooping and
rising again in great excitement.

" Mackerel ! " cried Ian.   " Where are the lines ? "

They found the fishing lines, let them run out behind
the boat and gave them both to Ann to hold, while they
rowed right into the stormy patch of sea.   The water
was thick with sprats, which were causing all the confusion on the surface.   The gulls were after the sprats,
and so were the mackerel.   Ann soon felt violent jerks
on both lines at once and Ian took the oars while Sovra
helped to pull in the fish.   The dripping lines were
coiled onto the floorboards, and soon the fish broke the
surface, leaping and twisting, flashing silver-green in the
silver foam, and the two girls heaved them in over the
side of the boat.   Sovra fell on hers and grasped it round
the middle, avoiding the sharp back fin.   She pushed
her thumb between its jaws and jerked its head back ;
its neck broke and it hung limp.   Throwing it down
clear of the line, she turned to find Ann making feeble

grabs at her fish, which was bounding about over her feet. Sovra caught it and killed it quickly, and pulled the hooks free.

Then she looked at Ann, who was pink with annoyance.

" I've never had to kill my fish before," she said crossly. " I thought they died as soon as they got out of water."

Sovra was so surprised and pleased to know more about fishing than Ann that she made no reply, but merely handed one line across for Ann to let out again.

" No thank you," said Ann. " I don't want them bleeding all over me. I'll go up in the bows."

She clambered past Ian, and sat on the mooring rope, looking sternly away from the others. Sovra smiled and went on fishing, then Ian did some fishing and Sovra rowed for a while until they changed places for her to have another turn with the mackerel. The boat was still in the middle of the shoal, and fish grabbed the hooks as soon as they were thrown out. In they came, tumbling silver bodies with green and black patterns on them, and the heap in the bottom of the boat grew bigger and there were gleaming scales all over the hair and arms and clothes of the two fishers, and bright red blood on their hands. The water that had splashed in with the fish was tinged with red, and swirled from side to side as the boat lilted on the waves.

" That's enough ! " cried Ian at last, as Sovra paused to wipe her face with her sleeve. " We'll never eat all those."

" Och, wasn't it thrilling, though," she exclaimed, looking back at the shoal they were leaving. " The way they pulled at the line as soon as it hit the water, almost. I wish we could throw them all back and do it again ! "

Ian laughed, but in the middle of the laugh a huge wave took the boat and tossed it sideways, and he spun off the seat into the pile of mackerel. Sovra caught the oars as he let go of them, and managed to push the nose of the boat round into the next wave. The boat lifted and shuddered and came to a stop, wallowing like a bison in a mudhole.

" Come on," said Ian, climbing up again covered with scales. " We'll both have to row round here."

Sovra found to her surprise that they were level with the westerly point of Fionn-ard, where the waves came jostling in from the open sea. They were short steep waves, and the boat had hardly time to ride over one before the next had caught it under the bows and was bouncing it up again. Every third or fourth wave was bigger than the rest, and the boat climbed steeply and swayed on the top for a moment before it dipped its nose and slid down as if it meant to dive to the bottom. Ian and Sovra rowed with their chins on their shoulders, judging the time to pull, for between waves their oars were right out of the water.

They had forgotten Ann, so fierce was the struggle, and they hardly thought where they were going, so intent were they on the endless heave and dip of the waves. At last Ian glanced at Fionn-ard, and shouted,

" We'll have to cross the point now. Turn her as

quick as you can. Don't let her be sideways on longer
than you can help."

He swung his oar over, so that they were both rowing
on the same side, and they pulled the boat round until it
was set on its course for the shore. As it turned broadside
on to the waves it lurched and wallowed most perilously,
the gunwales smacking the water on each side. For a
moment it seemed that the next big wave would roll it
right over, but before that arrived the boat was turned,
and the waves were banging at its stern and sending it
towards the shore.

Ian changed his oar back again, and rowed two
strokes to get the boat steady, then he leaned on the oar
and said breathlessly,

" Rest a bit, Sovra. The sea's taking us there now.
Let's have some chocolate."

" Good idea," said Sovra, and pulled out a damp slab
of chocolate from the haversack in the stern. She took
some herself, and broke off a large lump to put in Ian's
mouth, as he seemed disinclined to make the effort of
putting out a hand.

" In my *mouth*," said Ian. " I don't eat with my
nose."

" If your mouth didn't bounce up and down so, I
could hit it easily," said Sovra, leaning back and swaying
with the lurching of the waves. She had already hit
his nose and one eye, and ended with a dab at his
chin, before he snapped at the chocolate like a seal
catching fish, and managed to catch it between his
teeth.

" Did you know," he said indistinctly, " that the

Burmese executed people by hitting them under the chin ? "

" No," said Sovra. " Here's some for Ann."

While the boat had been making the perilous journey round the point, Ann had been clinging to the bows and trying to persuade herself that she was liking it. At first the waves seemed too small to bother about, but when the boat began to heave and lurch helplessly it became alarming. The boat seemed to stay in the same place for hours, at the mercy of those endless green ridges, that heaved up one after the other unceasingly. When the boat turned sideways on, Ann had to dig her nails into the wood to stop herself calling out. She was convinced that they were all going to be swallowed up in this relentless sea, miles from any hope of rescue, and their bones would be cast up on desolate western shores where nobody would ever find them. By the time they were heading inshore she had given up trying to be brave and was hiding her face on her clenched hands and heaving limply from side to side with the swing of the waves. She looked up when Ian spoke to Sovra, and saw the waves dashing against the rocks ahead, and then Ian held out to her a sticky bit of chocolate with fish scales on it, and the sight of it and the thought of the Burmese executioners, and a sudden convulsive twitching of the dead mackerel at her feet, were altogether too much for her. She gave a despairing wail, that rang out above the noise of the sea, and hung over the bows as limp as wet seaweed.

" My sorrow," said Ian. " She's being sick. Take my oar, Sovra."

He swung round and caught the back of Ann's mackintosh, afraid that she might fall right out. After a moment she slithered back onto the bottom of the boat, looking green and desperate. She put her hands over her face, and from behind them came a muffled cry,

" I wish I was *dreaming* all this ! "

" Oh, come on," said Ian. " Cheer up. It's horrid being seasick, but it's not far now."

" I thought you'd been sailing a lot," called Sovra over her shoulder, although she knew it was rather a mean thing to say.

" I *have*," said Ann indignantly. " But on a decent sea, not beastly steep waves like these."

She sat up straighter and wiped the spray from her face, which was a little less green. Ian smiled encouragingly, and to his surprise she went quite red, and said hurriedly,

" I haven't done *much* sailing, you know. I don't really know much about it. Anyway, you're much better at boats than I am, and I was frightened as well as sick. I'd never dare to row out into a rough sea like that."

" Och, yes, you would if you were used to it," Ian replied, rather taken aback by her sudden meekness, though he was pleased that she had stopped being superior for once.

" Come and sit back here," said Sovra. " It doesn't swing up and down as much as the front."

Ann clambered past her and sat down limply in the stern, not even bothering to point out that the front of the boat should be called the bows. The other two looked tactfully into the distance, and pulled for the shore with quick strokes. The waves sent the boat in with great surges, and soon it was in the more sheltered water of the little bay that was enclosed by the western points of Fionn-ard. Here was the beach of smooth white sand that Sovra had discovered from the cliffs above. The tide was high, but there was a good stretch of sand above the high-water-mark ; soft dry sand speckled with shells.

The boat was beached and the haversacks taken out, and the three explorers found a sheltered place between two spurs of rock. Here they stood for a moment looking out to sea.

Near them broke the green and silver foam, and beyond it surged the waves, green and blue in the sunlight, and far away the islands floated between the gleaming water and the clear pallor of the sky.

Ann took a deep breath, and turned to the other two.

" I'm sorry I've been so silly," she said. " I always pretend I know everything, but I don't really. I wish I was like you."

They looked at her in surprise, and then laughed in a friendly way.

" Well, you do know a lot," said Ian. " But you don't know about Fionn-ard. Would you like us to tell you about it ? "

10. *Mysterious Visitors*

"DON'T FEEL YOU'VE GOT to be nice to me, just because I was sick," said Ann, as they all sat down on the sand. " I didn't mean to be sick, but those fish gave me the shivers, the way they suddenly jumped."

"That's their nerves," said Ian. " They go on twitching quite a long while after they're dead."

"Oh," said Ann, as if she had just thought of something.

"What?"

"Well, you probably know about fish, but Daddy never leaves his in the sun. It makes them go all hard. Those mackerel in the boat are right in the sun. It would be a shame if they were spoiled."

"Och, yes!" cried Sovra, jumping up. "I'll put some seaweed over them. Good thing you reminded us, Ann."

She darted down to the rocks at the water's edge, and pulled off enough seaweed to cover the heap of mackerel in the boat. Ann was relieved to see that the others didn't mind being told about it, but she decided to make a great effort and stop being superior, even if she did see them doing silly things.

" What were you going to tell me ? " she asked, as they settled down to their sandwiches.

" About our shicling," said Ian.

" You mean your camping place ? "

" Yes.   What's the matter ? "

She hesitated, looking out at the bright sea, and then she said hurriedly,

" It's not fair to let you tell me.   I've been there and seen it.   I found it out yesterday."

" So it *was* you ! " cried Sovra.   " We thought it must have been."

" Did you know I'd been there, then ? " Ann asked, puzzled.   " You were on that island all the time.   You couldn't have seen me."

" Did you pick up a coat that was lying on the floor ? " said Ian.

" Oh . . . yes, I think I did."

" I knew I'd left it on the floor, and when I saw it hanging up I knew somebody must have been in."

" But *how* did you get there ? " asked Sovra.

" Across the stepping stones in the bog."

" *What ?* "

Ann nodded, looking almost excited, and said,

" Didn't you know about them ? "

" No.   Did you just find them ? "

" We looked for a way across, but there wasn't a sign of one."

" It's hard to see, even when you know where it is," said Ann.   " Old Donald told Mother that there was a way across."

" The old skellum," cried Ian. " He never told us, even when he knew we were living in the shieling."

" I don't think he wanted to tell Mother, but he didn't know she'd tell anyone who would actually go across by it."

Ann told them how she had seen the path from the top of Ben Shian, and how she had marked the spot where it began.

" Yesterday morning," she went on, " I waited till I could see you on that island, then I left Mother sketching and dashed off to the bog. It was madly terrifying, of course. I managed to find the first stone ; it had a lot of moss over it but it was quite firm. They're big square blocks of stone, just far enough apart to reach if you walk with a big stride. There's water or mud over all of them, but not much. They twist about all over the place. I got across and rushed up the hill and over, to where I'd seen your smoke that day Ian fell and bashed his head."

" You saw the smoke ? " exclaimed Sovra. " Oh dear, I never thought of that. Anyone could see it. Ian, why did we ever think we were hidden there ? "

" Why don't we ever have any sense ? " said Ian. " Go on, Ann."

" Oh, I just went in and looked at everything, but I didn't interfere with anything. It *did* look wizard. But I didn't stay long in case you came back. I ploughed across the bog again and found Mother running round in small circles looking for me. I didn't mean to let you know I'd been there, but I never thought you'd want me to know about it."

" Will you show us the way across ? " asked Ian.

" Of course I will. How do you get there ? Do you have to go right round to the village ? "

" No, there's a way in this side. We'll show you that too, if you like."

" It's rather hair-raising," said Sovra.

" Oh," said Ann, looking at Ian. " Is it anything to do with the waterfall ? "

" How did you know that ? "

" You said something about the waterfall after you'd hit your head that time."

" Ian," said Sovra accusingly.

" Och, how could I help saying things I shouldn't, after a dunt like that ? Yes, it's under the waterfall."

" How madly appalling," said Ann, alarmed.

" Ann," said Sovra suddenly. " What did you do with the boots ? "

Ann looked blankly at her.

" What boots ? "

" You didn't hide any, or take them away ? "

" Of course not. What do you mean ? Have you lost some ? "

Sovra and Ian stared at each other. They had solved the mystery of the coat that hung itself up, but the disappearance of the boots was more baffling than ever.

" There's somebody else who knows that path," said Sovra at last. " There must be."

" Donald knows about it," said Ann.

" No, it can't be Donald. He can't walk a step, and he'd not go taking boots. It must be someone from Lochhead."

"Nobody else knows," said Ann firmly. "Donald told Mother that the path had been lost for years. He's the only one. Besides, would anyone in Lochhead want those awful old boots of yours, Ian? You've probably shoved them out of sight somewhere and forgotten where."

Ian took a large mouthful of cake, and tried to speak decisively through it. The others waited until he had finished choking, then they dusted the crumbs off themselves and prepared to listen, for he looked as if his brain was working at great speed.

"Listen now," he said rather indistinctly, "It can't be Donald. And I don't believe anyone could find the path by accident. We looked as hard as bloodhounds and didn't see a sign of it. No, it's someone that knows. And another thing, Ann, is that they didn't take *my* boots. They took another pair, even older, that we found in the shieling."

"Well, whose were those? Or don't you know?"

"Those," said Ian, looking out to sea and frowning, "belonged to Alastair Gunn."

"He's the chieftain of this bit of land," said Sovra, before Ann could ask about him. "Or rather, he would be, but he was drowned, months ago——"

"Years ago," said Ian.

"Is it as long as that? Well, anyway, he's dead and the house is empty. He used to stay at Kindrachill, and he built the shieling we're living in now."

"Kindrachill?" exclaimed Ann.

"Yes. That's the name of the house. What are you looking for?"

Ann scuffled about in the haversack where the sand-

wiches had been, and pulled out a square of folded newspaper. She had folded it herself, for it had been crumpled up and looked untidy.

" That's the bit I shoved in there yesterday," said Ian.
" We were reading the advertisements."

" It says something about Kindrachill. I noticed
it just now. I knew I'd heard the name before."

They waited eagerly while she read quickly down one
column.

" This says it is going to be sold," she said. " The
whole estate. Because of the mortgage."

" What on earth is a mortgage ? " asked Sovra.

" I don't quite know, but I think it's when you borrow
money and say you'll give your house if you can't pay
the money back. It says here that the mortgage is due
to foreclose at Michaelmas, and it seems certain that the
present owner can't pay, so whoever's got the mortgage
is going to sell the house and get his money that way."

" My sorrow," said Ian restlessly. " It will be bought
by some horrible rich old man for the shooting. Oh,
Sovra, isn't it beastly ? All the decent people going,
and hundreds of deserted villages all over the place.
And now Kindrachill's got to be sold, and the Gunns
have been there for centuries."

He rubbed his hands distressfully over the dry soft
sand, and the sand responded with a faint singing whine,
as if it were sorry too. Ian laughed, suddenly forgetting
about Kindrachill, and they all started to make the sand
sing.

" Listen ! " said Sovra, starting up. " There's some
music somewhere."

" Out there," said Ann, and pointed to a big motor launch that had come in sight, making for Melvick. It was a long way out, but the wind brought the sound of dance music clearly over the water.

" Horrible," said Ian. " You see what I mean ? They're some of the rich people who come up here, and they don't know any better than to go up and down with a wireless shrieking all the time."

" It's been going up and down for days," said Ann. " We saw it in Melvick when we arrived here, with lots of frightfully rich-looking people on it."

" *They'll* not see any seals or porpoises or anything else, with that noise going on," said Sovra.

The launch drew rapidly away, passed behind Castle Island and disappeared in the direction of Melvick. The three children sighed with relief as it went, and listened to the quietness that was broken only by the wind and waves and seagulls.

" It's time we were going," said Sovra reluctantly.

" If Ann shows us the stepping-stones, we won't have to fit in with the tide," said Ian. " We can only do the waterfall way when the tide's fairly high, you see."

" Of course, so we won't," said Sovra. " I hadn't realized that. Ann, are you going to be all right going back round the point ? "

They looked at the waves, which were still quick and furious against the rocky headland, and Ann turned a little pale.

" Well, I've got to get back somehow," she said. " Won't it be easier going back ? "

" We'll have the wind with us," said Ian.   " But the
tide's turned, so it will be against us.   Would you rather
not ? "

" Oh, don't be silly.   I can't stay here for days
waiting for it to calm down."

" You needn't," said Ian.   " There is a way up the
cliff.   We found it the other day.   You can go over the
hill and down to the shieling, and we'll go round and
join you."

Ann was obviously relieved to hear this, and said she
could easily manage the climb which they showed her.
The rock was broken, and scored across by narrow ledges, which made climbing easy for anyone who didn't
mind heights.   Ann was as good at climbing as she was at
most other things, and the other two watched her pull
herself quickly up the cliff and gain the sloping grass
above.

The homeward journey by sea was easier than they
expected, partly because the boat was less heavily laden,
and partly because the wind was helping them more
than the tide hindered them.   The boat bounced up and
down like a cork, and rode the waves with short jerks
and dips and lurches, and even Sovra began to feel
uneasy inside, but soon the point was rounded, and they
reached the calmer waters of Loch Fionn.

Ann reached the top of the ridge above the hollow, and
followed it round so that she could see the boat.   She
shuddered as the waves tossed it about, and felt very
thankful to be on dry land.   The two oarsmen seemed
to be enjoying their rough ride ; she could hear bursts
of breathless singing in the lulls of the wind.   Soon she

could hear the roar of the waterfall ahead, and could see the stream leaping down from the higher rocks towards it. She climbed down to the edge of the cliff and peered over, for the boat was drawing in towards the shore, out of sight of the top of the ridge.

Ian saw her and waved. Sovra told him sternly to mind where he was going, and he started telling her about stormy petrels, which were called after St. Peter because they ran along the surface of the water. But he rowed as he talked, and the boat swung neatly round beyond the whirlpool and shot in behind the waterfall. Ann leaned further over, wondering whether they were all right, but after a minute she heard voices behind her, coming up out of the ground. She got up and ran towards the sound, and saw Sovra rising up from a patch of heather, followed by Ian, still talking hard.

" Gosh, I'm glad I wasn't with you," said Ann. " Doesn't it give you the *absolute* shivers ? "

" It's not so bad really," said Sovra. " We keep right outside the current."

" There's the shieling," said Ian, looking down at it with satisfaction.

" I wonder if anyone's been there," said Sovra.

" We should have tied black cotton across the doorway," said Ian. " Then if it was broken, we'd know someone had."

" Have you got any black cotton ? " Ann asked.

" Och, no. Don't be so practical."

" Come on, do let's find the stepping-stones," said Sovra impatiently.

They ran down and across the hollow, jumping the burn just where it ran out of the lochan, and up the far side through the trees, giving the shieling a glance as they passed. It looked quite undisturbed, and the hollow was so sheltered and still that you would have said nobody had entered it for years.

Ann led the way, straight up and over the wooded ridge, and down the steep rocky slope beyond. She climbed down this as fast as she could, trying to show that she was good at climbing in spite of being bad at boats. The other two kept up easily, however, and were hardly out of breath when they reached the bottom.

"Be careful here," said Ann. "The bog begins straight away. The path starts over there by that bush."

"Juniper," said Ian, as they came to the bush she had indicated.

"Or bog myrtle," said Sovra.

"I bet it's juniper. Where's the first stone ?"

"Just there, about a yard in," said Ann, pointing at the mud and weeds that lay dank and slimy before them. Ian nodded, took a confident stride, and sank in right up to his thigh.

"No, *not* there," cried Ann.

"So it isn't," said Ian. "My sorrow, I'm stuck."

Ann jumped onto the stone, which was hidden under the rushes just beside him, and tried to pull him out. Sovra joined her—there was room for two people to stand very close on the stone. Ian found the next stepping-stone, and managed to heave himself out onto it. The mud let go of his leg with a reluctant sucking gurgle, and Sovra shuddered.

"For heaven's sake be careful," said Ann. "If you look hard you can see the stones all right. Here, let me go first."

"No no," said Ian, and started off rapidly across the bog. Once you knew what to look for, the stones were easy to find, though at first there seemed to be nothing but mud and moss and undergrowth with no firmness to it. Ian stepped confidently from one stone to another, looking ahead for the flat patches of moss that showed where they were, and the two girls followed more slowly.

When they reached firm ground they looked back, and the bog seemed as impassable as ever.

"You couldn't do that in winter," said Sovra, squelching her toes in the mud that had filled her shoes.

"You could if you knew exactly where to tread. It's not really a dangerous bog," said Ian. "I'm terribly hungry. Let's go and have tea."

"Are you going across in the boat?" Ann asked.

"Yes, it'll be much quicker than going round by the road. Will you come? It's not really frightening going out by the waterfall," said Ian.

"Of course I'll come. If you're not frightened by it, I won't be," said Ann rather coldly.

They recrossed the bog and ran back through the hollow. Ann was excited by the narrow way down into the cave, and would have asked a lot of questions about it if she hadn't been so busy looking where she was going.

When they reached the cave, she stood for a moment in the cold darkness, listening to the thunder of the water-fall and watching the wavering gleams of light on the rock. It was a little alarming to think of venturing out into the noise and fury of the whirlpool, but Ann got into the boat without hesitating. The others weren't afraid, and she didn't want them to think she was.

" Hold tight," shouted Ian as they pushed off.

The boat slid out, gave a sudden heave, and rocked sideways into calmer water. Ann looked over the gun-wale, and saw the rock rising up under them. The boat crossed the sunk reef with a gentle grating noise, and reached deep water, too deep to see the bottom.

" Just in time," said Sovra. " We'll have to come back across the stepping stones."

They reached Camas Ban in time for tea, and tried to wash off some of the mud before Mr. and Mrs. Paget saw them.

" If there's anything anywhere to fall off or into or over, Ian always *does* fall," said Sovra, as they all dabbled their feet in the bath. Ann looked at Ian's legs, one brown and bare, the other coated with black mud, and giggled. Ian set to work with a nailbrush, pausing only to say,

" Did you know that turtles have three hearts ? "

Sovra shared Ann's towel, and began to feel quite friendly towards her. Being seasick seemed to have made her nicer. Ann herself began to hope that they might ask her to come over to the shieling again and do some cooking for them. She was longing to see more of this exciting country, and had quite forgotten how boring she had found it at first.

" Ah, dear children ! " said Mrs. Paget, as tea began. " Have you had a happy little day ? "

As they had all just taken their first large mouthful, there was no answer, but Ann grinned and nodded as hard as she could.

" Telephone," said Mrs. Kennedy. Her husband got up with a deep sigh, remarking,

" Never expect to be a doctor *and* have any meals. It just can't be done," but before he reached the door, Agnes, the girl who helped, opened it and hissed,

" It is for Mrs. Paget. From Glasgow."

Mrs. Paget exclaimed brightly and sped out, her beads clashing round her. After some time she came back, looking even more excited.

" Oh, you dear people ! " she cried. " I shall have to leave you straight away. I'm *so* sorry, but it is such a chance."

" What is ? " asked Mr. Paget, going on calmly with his tea.

" They want me to go to Glasgow and do a one man show of all the sketches I've done here," she said breathlessly. " Such a chance ! I must go at once, though. Tomorrow. I feel so dreadful, being so sudden with you dear people, but it must be done."

" That sounds most satisfactory," said Dr. Kennedy with real admiration. " Congratulations."

" You'd better take Ann," said Mr. Paget. " I don't want her, and she doesn't want to be on her own here."

" Certainly, my dear Annabel shall come too. Of course she shall."

Ann looked at her with startled eyes, and went very red. Then suddenly she got up and ran out of the room.

" Now what on earth . . . ? " said her father.

" Perhaps she wants to stay," said Mrs. Kennedy.

" Oh, but it would be so lonely for her without me," said Mrs. Paget, bewildered. " Why did she run away like that ? "

Ian went to the door, which opened into the sitting room. He saw Ann standing by the window, staring out and chewing her handkerchief. Her shoulders were heaving. He sat down again and murmured very quietly to Sovra beside him.

" For heaven's sake, take her with you," said Mr. Paget. " You know how she hates hanging around by herself."

Sovra looked at Ian, and they both started talking together. Dr. Kennedy put his hands over his ears.

" One at a time," he exclaimed.

" Couldn't she come and camp with us ? " said Sovra, while Ian nodded eagerly.

Ann's parents looked doubtful. Mrs. Kennedy started wondering about camp-beds. Dr. Kennedy looked surprised and pleased.

Ian saw the look of relief that was mixed with Mr. Paget's doubt, and knew that it was as good as settled, although there would have to be all sorts of polite questions of the " are you sure you don't mind ? " type first. And settled it was very speedily.

" After all, it would be a pity to take dear

Annabel away from all this air and freshness," said Mrs. Paget.

" She can do your cooking and make herself useful," said Mr. Paget.

" You can take the other camp bed back with you," said Mrs. Kennedy.

" It's about time you shared some of the things you're lucky enough to have," said Dr. Kennedy sternly.

By the time Ann came back, rather red about the eyes, everything was arranged. She looked even more upset when she heard what was going to happen, but this time it was because she could hardly believe in her good luck. Dr. Kennedy was surprised to see that she really wanted to stay, and thought that perhaps Ian and Sovra wouldn't find her a nuisance after all.

" Why not let her go tonight ? " suggested Mr. Paget eventually. " Then she'll be out of the way while you pack your pictures."

" Oh ! " said Ann breathlessly, and looked out at the calm evening. " That would be absolutely *super* wizard. Could I really ? "

" Why not ? " said Mrs. Kennedy. " You might as well make the most of the fine evening. It's sure to rain tomorrow."

After tea there was an hour or so of bustle and turmoil, as Mrs. Paget started packing, and Mrs. Kennedy found extra blankets, and Ann shoved her clothes into a suitcase, and the two men got out of the way and talked about fish. Soon, however, everything was ready, and Ann said good-bye to her mother, who kissed her as if she was setting out for the South Pole. The boat moved heavily out of the white-sanded bay, and across the calming water of Loch Fionn.

" Oh, this is wonderful," said Ann. " I really won't be a bother. Would you like me to do the cooking for you ? "

" Yes, do if you like it," said Sovra. " I usually get fed up with it. I'm afraid your clothes will get a bit messy."

" That doesn't matter," said Ann, looking at the muddy splashes on her yellow shorts. " I'll mend yours, if you like."

" Och, you haven't got to be useful all the time," said Ian.

They took the boat into the landing place on the inland side of the bog, and transported its cargo safely across the stepping-stones and down to the shieling.

" Put the bed along the wall under the window," said Sovra, taking charge. " Ian, you hang a blanket in front of your bed. That's your bedroom behind it. We'll have the rest of the room for ours."

Ian fixed a blanket as a bed-curtain and crawled in behind it.

" It's like a sarcophagus," he said. " All dark and stuffy."

" Well, you needn't have it right along. Come and help with the camp-bed."

There was not much room to move about when the second bed was up, but Ann thought she had never been in such an exciting house. Sovra lit the fire, and the flames sent bright gleams into the shadowy corners.

" I saw the smoke that day Ian fell over the rock," Ann reminded them.

" So you did. I'd lighted it to make some tea because Ian was feeling so uncouth," said Sovra. " It was the first time we had a fire here."

" There's the Gunn crest," said Ian, pointing to the hearth-stone. " A spray of juniper."

" What are you having for breakfast ? " said Ann, becoming practical.

" Och, it's too early to think about that," said Ian.

" Well, I just wondered if you wanted porridge."

" It takes too long to cook, or we would have it."

Ann laughed at their ignorance in a kind way that was not annoying, and put some oatmeal in water to soak overnight. Then she set to work on Ian's jersey, mending the hole in the elbows and the thin places under the arms. The others lit candles and sat and watched her, and outside it grew darker and darker as the sun sank.

" The wind's rising again," said Sovra.

" Is it ? It was much calmer just now," said Ian.

" The trees are rustling. Listen."

They listened, and heard the stirring of branches in the dusk outside, then silence.

" That's not the wind," said Ian, and something in his voice sent a shiver down Ann's back.

" What do you mean ? What else could it be ? "

" Sheep," said Sovra doubtfully.

" There aren't any sheep," said Ian.

" Was it somebody coming through the trees ? " asked Ann, trying not to feel alarmed.

There was a sound outside the window, and for a moment the darkening sky was blotted out as something moved across towards the door. Ian and Sovra stared at the door, hardly breathing, and Ann clutched her sewing things and felt quite scared.

There was a gentle knock, and the door was pushed open. Someone was standing there, so dark against the sunset that his face could not be seen. After a second he said, without moving,

"May I come in? My name's Alastair Gunn."

11. *The Return of the Chieftain*

THERE WAS A SECOND OF
silence, and nobody moved. Ian and Sovra were
convinced, for half that second, that it was Alastair's
ghost, but Ann had been brought up in a common-sense
English town, and didn't ever think about ghosts.

"What?" she exclaimed. "You? The chieftain
of Kindrachill?"

"But you were drowned," said Sovra, and drew in her
breath with a sudden gasp.

"Come in, do," said Ian, feeling brave again.

The man stepped forward, leaning on a stick, and the
door swung shut behind him. As he came into the
candle-light and fire-light they saw that he was not very
big, though in the darkness against the sky he had looked
like a giant. He was thin and fair, and he walked with
a limp.

"I wasn't drowned," he said, in a soft Highland voice
that suddenly made Ann recognize him.

"Oh, you're the man on the motor-bike!" she cried.
"Come and sit down, won't you?"

"Thank you," he said, and sat down on the floor
beside her. "I'm sorry if I startled you. I've been
to call on you by daylight, but you were never here when
I came."

181

The other two had begun to take in the fact that this was really the long-lost Alastair, quite undrowned, and suddenly they found all sorts of questions and exclamations rushing into their minds and out of their mouths before they could stop them.

" It was you who came for the boots," said Ian. " You're wearing them now."

" We saw your footprints on the sand," said Sovra.

" Does Donald know you're here ? "

" Have you come to live in Kindrachill ? "

" When did you come here and not find us ? "

" When did Ann meet you ? "

" Why did people think you were drowned ? "

" Do you want some supper ? " said Ann as the others paused for breath.

Alastair looked at them all in turn, then he laughed rather awkwardly and answered,

" I'd no idea you knew such a lot about me."

" Donald told us a bit about you," said Ian.   " Please tell us about him first—does he know you're all right ? "

" Yes, I've been to see him.   If I'd realized he'd heard a rumour that I was drowned I'd have tried to let him know long ago, but I never imagined it would penetrate up here, or that he would even remember me. It's years since I was here last."

" That was when I met him," said Ann.   " He was going to see Donald and he gave me a lift on his motorbike.   It was the day I tried to chase you in bare feet, and I scraped my heel and was limping, and that's why he stopped, because he had a fellow-feeling."

" And you never knew who he was ? " exclaimed Ian.

" No. How could I ? "

" Well, don't talk about him as if he wasn't here," said Sovra. " Please would you like some supper ? "

" No, thank you very much. I've had some. That's why I'm as late as this. I thought you'd be bound to be here in the evening."

" What did you want to see us for ? " asked Ian, his heart suddenly sinking. " Do you want us to go away from here ? "

" Why on earth should I ? "

" Well, it's your house," said Sovra, looking at the crest carved on the hearthstone. Alastair looked at it too, and smiled.

" Yes, it's still mine, but I've no objection to you living in it. I certainly didn't come here to turn you out. No, I wanted to see you because I thought you might let me camp here a bit with you while I interview various people. There's not a room to be had for miles. I've been at a Youth Hostel on Loch Duich, but it's too far away to be much use."

" Oh ! " said Ian with awe. " Would you really come here with us ? "

" I don't think I'd better. You're pretty crowded in here as it is. I thought it was just two boys camping. I don't want to be a nuisance."

" Och, you *must* come here, and we'll go," said Sovra. " We can't keep you out of your own house."

" Can't you stay here tonight, anyway ? " Ann suggested. " It's getting awfully dark, and you might fall into the bog if you went back. Sovra and I can sleep on that big shelf, and you and Ian can have the beds. There's plenty of room."

She talked as if she had taken charge of everything, but the others didn't mind. All they wanted was to get Alastair to stay as long as possible.

" I'll see," said Alastair. " But first of all——"

" Oh, *please* tell us why——" Sovra began, but he cut her short, pleasantly but firmly.

" I know there are dozens of questions you want answered, but I'd like some of mine answered first. To begin with, how did you get here ? "

They told him how they had been carried in under the waterfall and had found the house quite by accident, and then Ann described how she had found the stepping-stones, and after that Ian told him what Donald had said about him, and after that they all sat silent with questions ready to burst out at the first opportunity.

" I see," said Alastair. " I *am* sorry about Donald. When I went to see him the other day I was expecting to find he'd quite forgotten me. I was rather shaken to be greeted as a ghost and then nearly wept over. I *did* feel bad about it, though it wasn't really my fault."

" *Please* tell us what really happened to you," said Sovra, and the others nodded and stared at him imploringly.

" Oh, I just got lost, that's all."

" Lost ? Where ? "

" Somewhere in the Pacific. It's quite a good place to get lost in, you know, especially if you're flying all alone and your compass suddenly packs up and your

petrol begins to give out.   When that happens, you make
for the nearest island without bothering about its latitude
and longitude.   At least, that's what I did, not being
as good a swimmer as all that."

" Was it a desert island ? " Sovra asked.

" Oh no, full of natives.   Good types in their way.
They came and collected me off the reef where I landed,
and were very friendly and all that, but as I couldn't
speak a word of their language nor they of mine, there
wasn't much progress.   So there I stayed."

" How *did* you get away, then ? " asked Ian.

" Well, after a bit I picked up a few words, and the
foot I'd wrecked on that reef got a bit more serviceable,
and I persuaded some of the braver ones to take me in a
canoe to a bigger island, where a steamer called about
once every other blue moon.   It was a bit of a bind
having to wait for it, but I couldn't communicate with
anyone, so I just had to sit there and learn how to make
flower necklaces.   However, at last a steamer came, and
I reported back to the authorities, who said I'd been
officially drowned for months and I'd better go home or
it would put all their records wrong.   So home I
came——"

" Did they really say that ? " asked Sovra.

" No, of course not," said Alastair.   " They were very
decent and even seemed pleased to see me, but they said
I'd have to come home because of my foot.   They con-
sidered me pretty useless, though I can get about quite
easily.   So I sent telegrams to a few distant relatives
who'd probably forgotten my existence, and if I'd
remembered old Donald I'd have sent him one too,

though it never occurred to me that he'd hear about it, or care much if he did."

"Well, it wasn't your fault that he did," said Ian. "You couldn't possibly help it. He only heard of it by accident, and he told us, but nobody else up here knew until he told them."

"Well, anyway, I came home, feeling that there wasn't much future in being a cripple with no means of earning a living, and when I got home I found that I was the heir to a place I couldn't afford to keep, and there's not much future in that either."

"Didn't you know you'd inherited it when Colonel Gunn died?"

"Yes, but I never had a chance to come up here before I was sent out to the Pacific to get lost. I always assumed I'd be able to pay off the mortgage, too—or perhaps you don't know about that."

"Oh, yes, we do," said Ann. "I tried to explain to them what a mortgage was, but you probably know better than I do."

"It said in the papers that Kindrachill's got to be sold," said Ian anxiously, hoping to hear Alastair contradict it. But he only sighed and said,

"The papers are about right, I'm afraid. I've reckoned up everything I can lay my hands on, and I'm still five hundred pounds short. Unless I can raise that before the end of September, the whole estate will have to be sold. I came up to Glasgow to go into it, and that's how it is. Do you know why I came on up here?"

"Weren't you going to, anyway?" asked Sovra.

"No. I didn't see any point in it. But I happened

to go to a show of pictures—I'm rather keen on water colours, though I can't do it myself——"

Ann made a sudden movement, but nobody noticed, and he went on,

" —and there was one of the deserted village just down by the shore there. I recognised it at once, and when I looked at it closer I saw that there must be someone in this house. I'd clean forgotten about the house and the stepping-stones and everything, but when I saw the smoke rising up behind the hill——"

" I knew it ! " cried Ann. " Mother painted that picture. I saw her, and I saw the smoke. The day you hurt your head, Ian."

Ian got up, moving restlessly from one foot to the other.

" Was that why you came here ? " he asked.

" Yes. I thought the house might still be fit to live in, and I had a wild idea of keeping back Fionn-ard from the rest of the estate, and coming up here sometimes. Though as it happens I can't do that ; the whole lot has to go together."

" Then you came because we'd lit a fire," Ian said excitedly, and Sovra suddenly realized what he was driving at.

" It was the first fire we lighted on your own hearth-stone, Alastair," she said. " And it *did* bring you back. We wanted it to, but of course we thought it was no good."

" What are you talking about ? " cried Ann.

Alastair laughed, but it was such a kind laugh that Sovra knew he was not laughing at her, but because he was pleased.

" I'm glad you had such kind thoughts about me," he said. " I'd forgotten that old story. I suppose Donald told it to you ? "

" Yes, but it's come true, hasn't it ? "

" Not altogether," said Alastair, looking grave. " I shall have to go away again. I'm not back for good."

" Oh, I *wish* you were ! " cried Ian.

" Well, it can't be helped, and anyway it's not September yet. What's your name, by the way ? " he added, turning to Ann, who told him.

" Then Ann, do tell me why you're here too. I thought you were staying with Dr. Kennedy."

Ann blushed, remembering what she had said to him about the other two.

" I was, but Ian and Sovra have been awfully decent and let me come here, because my mother's gone away and my father didn't want me there just with him."

" It wasn't awful decency at all," said Ian. " You see, we'd been rather beastly to her. But it's all right now and she's going to cook for us."

" Oh, you will stay here tonight, won't you ? " said Ann, thinking about breakfast.

" Are you sure it wouldn't be a nuisance ? I've got some food with me, and a blanket. I can easily sleep outside."

" You'd get soaked if you did," said Sovra firmly. " Where have you left your things ? "

" Just this side of the bog. I'll go and collect them, it's not quite dark yet."

" Where's the torch ? " said Ian, jumping up. " I'll come and help you. It will be murky under the trees."

They set out at once, Ian holding the torch low so that they could both see where they were treading, and Alastair walking unevenly but at a good rate with the help of his stick.

" I say, we did ask an awful lot of questions," said Ian. " But we've been wondering about you ever since Donald told us about you, and we wanted to know everything straight away."

" Well, it's nice to know I wasn't completely forgotten. I have seen you before, of course, but I only remember one occasion when I actually spoke to you."

" Was that when we all went to the singing sands ? "

" Yes, I suppose that was it. We were all in a big boat. You were rather overcome, being with so many strangers, and I made some daft remark and you looked more overcome than ever."

" Well, you were an awful lot older than me—I suppose you still are, actually. I say ! "

" What ? "

They had reached the brow of the wooded ridge, and before them lay the dark shadows of the bog and the dusk of the hills beyond.

" The other night, I saw a light over there, straight over yonder. It must have been in Kindrachill, but I never realised it ! "

" Oh, I expect that was my lamp you saw. Rather late ? "

" I think so. I'd been asleep quite a bit before."

" Yes, I got into the house—I've got the key of the back door with me—and had a look round. I meant to stay there and camp out among the dust-sheets, but

I couldn't take it.   I just wandered round with a lamp for a bit, then went and found some hay in a barn to sleep in."

" It must be horrible, seeing it like that. Alastair, if you *do* have to sell it, won't you please come and stay with us sometimes ? Or wouldn't you want to come back at all ? "

" Thank you very much. I'll see how I feel, after September."

They had to stop talking here, and attend to the ground, for it fell away steeply, and was difficult for a lame man to manage. While they were doing this, the two girls were rearranging the shieling.

" Mother would be horrified," said Ann. " Only one little window, and four people sleeping inside. She says she always needs great draughts of fresh air."

" If it's draughts you want, leave the door open," said Sovra, busily counting blankets. " Do you kick much in your sleep ? "

" I don't think so. Do you ? "

" I always stay tucked in and tidy. Ian's awful, he kicks himself right out of his sleeping bag and everything."

" This bed's very wide, anyway," said Ann, looking at the built-in shelf. " It will be rather wizard with a curtain and all, like another little room. What are you doing ? "

" Just feeling all muddled," said Sovra, who was kneeling by the fire and sweeping the ashes away from the carving on the stone. " The return of the chieftain. We heard he was dead ages ago. It was sad, but everyone's forgotten about it. And now he's here, and we're making his bed and cooking porridge for him."

"I am, you mean." Ann went over to the porridge pan, and put an extra handful of oatmeal in to soak. "It's all very well for you Highlanders to sit about gazing soulfully into the fire. If it wasn't for me you'd never get any breakfast or anything."

"We wouldn't mind," said Sovra. "Ann, why did you sound so surprised when Alastair said who he was?"

"Well, he's not my idea of a chieftain."

"What d'you think a chieftain would look like?"

"Oh, a wizard huge man with red hair, dressed in tartan with broadswords and things, and lovely mournful Celtic eyes."

Sovra laughed.

"You *do* have daft ideas."

"Well, anyway, Alastair's not a bit like that."

"Yes—he's got sad eyes. Didn't you notice, when he said he'd have to go away again and let Kindrachill be sold? The more I think of it, the sadder it gets. I wish we could do something about it."

She got up and went to the door to see if the others were coming. The night was dark and cloudy, but between the clouds the stars shone palely down on the water of the lochan. Sovra heard footsteps in the wood, and Ian asking strings of questions about canoes. Alastair gave him an answer now and then, picking his way cautiously over the rough ground.

"I'll take that," said Sovra, running up and taking the blanket he was carrying. "You know, I wish we'd known you were coming. We could have come and met

you and said ' Welcome home, Gunn of Kindrachill,'
or something like that."

" Isn't that just like a *girl* ? " said Ian. " She's
getting all excitable."

" You poor natural," returned his sister with con-
tempt. " *Don't* tread there ! "

" Too late," said Ian, who had plunged through the
door of the shieling straight into a pile of tin plates.
These spun away beneath his feet with a clash and a
clatter, and Ann looked savagely at him as she went to
pick them up.

Alastair stood for a moment at the door, surveying
the muddle of bedclothes and shoes and books that
overflowed onto the floor from beds and table and cupboard.

" I'm sorry it's so untidy," said Ann, still annoyed.

" It doesn't worry me," Alastair replied. To take
her mind off the untidiness, he said,

" Talking of excitable women, Ian, I nearly killed one
the other day."

" Good thing too," said Ian.

" Hmf," said Sovra, unable to think of a good retort.

" Oh, I didn't mean to kill her," said Alastair. " I
was tearing along on my motor-bike—I was coming to
call on your parents, but they were both out—and there
was this weird female standing in the middle of the road,
round a blind corner. A sort of arty type in the widest
hat I've ever seen." Ann had gone very red, and the
other two were trying to find some way to stop him tactfully, but he went on,

" She was fearfully amused, as a matter of fact. Very

decent of her, but I must say it shook me. I missed her by inches. What are you all staring at? "

" That was Mother," said Ann. " She does look rather weird in her painting clothes."

" Oh my lord," said Alastair, horrified. " What an awful thing to go and say. I *am* sorry."

" That's all right," Ann assured him cheerfully. " I don't like that hat much either."

" But I ought to have known. You said it was your mother that painted the picture. What a fool I am."

" Oh, be quiet and have some cocoa," said Ann, who didn't seem to mind how she ordered him about. Alastair meekly took the cocoa she gave him and sat down on a stool.

" It's queer how you always missed us," said Sovra. " That was the day we went up Ben Shian and Mummy came to meet us."

" How long can you stay, anyway? " Ian asked.

" I'm not sure. I want to see some of the local people, to find out if they want to buy the houses they're in when the estate's sold. Then I'll have to go back to the lawyers in Glasgow. I can stay a few days here, anyway."

He looked at Ann and said with a smile,

" It's your mother I have to thank for bringing me up here, apparently."

" Because she painted the smoke? " said Sovra. " But it was us that lighted the fire."

" It was me that fell down and had to have a fire lit for me," said Ian.

" Well, it was me that chased you and made you fall down," said Ann.

" In that case, thank you all very much," said Alastair, and stared thoughtfully at the fire blazing on his own hearth.

12. *Treasure on the Island*

WHEN IAN WOKE NEXT MORN-
ing, the sun was rising, and bright daylight streamed in
and pointed out the confusion inside the shieling. It
shone on the crumpled heap of clothes at the end of the
built-in bed, which was all that could be seen of the two
girls still fast asleep behind their curtain. It lingered on
the dusty floor, where peat ash spread a grey film over
everything, and it shone on the back of Alastair's head,
half hidden under the blanket.

Ian sat up with a start of excitement, to find that he
had fought his way out of his sleeping bag and blankets
during the night. He felt energetic, and decided to go
and bathe before the others woke up.

The lochan was cold as night, for the sun had just
reached it and had not yet begun to warm it. Ian
threw off his pyjamas and plunged in before he lost
courage, splashing as hard as he could across to the other
side. When he climbed out and turned round, there was
Alastair in his pyjamas coming down from the shieling.
He could walk quite well without his stick, though he
limped much more and looked unsteady.

" I've not done this for years," he said with a shiver.
" Is it as cold as it looks ? "

" Yes, but it's lovely ! Come on."

He came on, and they splashed and swam until they were out of breath and warm again. By the time they got back to the shieling, the girls were up and breakfast nearly ready. Ann was having a lovely time, cooking porridge and arranging the breakfast-things and telling Sovra exactly what to do. Sovra did things in her own way, cheerfully saying " Yes " every now and then but not really listening to Ann at all.

After breakfast Alastair went off to see people, and the others accompanied him across the stepping-stones and waved good-bye as he went on into the wood. They went across the stepping-stones several times, to get to know them properly, and Ian slipped into the mud with both feet, and Ann got rather superior about it until they threatened to throw her in and watch the bubbles come up. After that she behaved better, and they had a lazy day on the shore, exploring the rocks and cliffs.

" Let's go and see if Alastair's coming," Sovra suggested, when they were beginning to feel like supper-time.

" D'you think we dreamed it all ? " said Ian.

" Come on and don't be silly," said Ann, and started briskly up the hill behind the shieling.

" Let's chase Ann," said Ian brightly, and set off in pursuit, but she had had a good start and ran very fast through the twisted oak trees. The other two caught up with her at the top of the ridge where the trees ended, and threw themselves panting on the grass. There was no sign of Alastair on the open ground between them and the railway embankment, and no sound of a motor-bike either.

" I hope he is going to come back," said Sovra.

" Perhaps he's decided to go back to Glasgow, or wherever it is that he lives."

" I wonder where he *does* live and what he does there," said Ann. " He hardly told us anything like that. Ian was asking so many silly questions about catamarans this morning that nobody else could get a word in edgeways."

" Shut up, Sassenach," said Ian in his most annoying voice.

" Shut up yourself," said Sovra. " You needn't get all conceited now you've got Alastair to talk to. You weren't so despising about girls before he arrived."

" I have to put up with women when there's nobody else. Andromeda, I'll race you across the hollow and up to that rock."

" If you go on calling me silly names, I'll call Sovra primrose," said Ann, getting up crossly.

" Oh, Ian, why on earth did you tell her that ? " his sister demanded.

" I'd forgotten I had. It must have been after that bump on the head."

" You always make excuses," said Ann. " But you *are* being disagreeable."

" My sorrow, listen to that ! Come on, race me."

He tried to make her run down the hill again, but she shook his hand off her arm and darted off by herself. Ian gave a loud halloo and rushed after her, and Sovra followed, almost as cross with him as Ann was. It was bad enough being called ' primrose ', without having your own brother telling people about it.

Ann stopped by the lochan and started hurling stones

into it. Ian jumped across the burn lower down, and she threw a stone just short of him so that he got splashed. "Ho-ro, Angelica," shouted Ian. "I can do that too," and he flung another to splash her. Sovra joined in from further along, and soon a three-cornered battle was raging, and showers of spray came spinning up from the little lochan. Ann was furious ; her eyes flashed and she was red in the face, and when her plaits swung forward she flung them back savagely. Sovra was annoyed with both the others, but she aimed her splashes at Ian because he had been getting so despising about girls. Ian himself was thoroughly enjoying it all ; he couldn't resist making people cross sometimes, it was so exciting to see them getting all worked up.

They shouted as they threw the stones, and the quiet hollow resounded with voices and splashing. The sun was sinking in a clear golden sky above them, and there were rainbows in the spray all round them, but they never noticed, and they had forgotten all about Alastair and supper-time.

Suddenly Ian stood still with his mouth open, and the other two turned to see what he was staring at. They found Alastair leaning on his stick just behind them, looking tired and annoyed. Sovra realized that it was his green hollow, his quaich, they were shouting and fighting in, and felt ashamed and sorry for him. Before she could say anything, though, Ann darted past her and cried,

"Oh, Alastair, Ian's been so beastly ! He won't do a thing but make fun of us."

"Och, *I* don't mind that," said Sovra quickly.

" But honestly, he's been awful all day——" Ann went on.

" Stop binding, for heaven's sake," said Alastair patiently. " Don't you think we'd better go and have some supper ? "

" Supper ! " Ann cried, horrified that she had forgotten about it. She turned and ran towards the shieling, and Sovra followed her, hoping that there was something nice to give Alastair. He looked as if he needed cheering up.

" I cooked the mackerel this morning, so they only need hotting up," said Ann busily. " Oh dear, I'm soaked."

" So'm I. Let's put on our pyjamas and a jersey. It's quite warm in here."

They hurried to get supper ready, forgetting how angry they had been with each other, and Ann went so far as to say that she realized Sovra couldn't help her name and it wasn't fair to laugh at it.

" Mother nearly called me Persephone," she admitted, " but Father wouldn't let her. It would have been hectically appalling if she had."

The table was set, and the mackerel sizzling by the fire, and buttered toast soaking into a warm sogginess, before the other two appeared. Alastair came in first, looking rather anxious, and Ian sidled in behind him, trying furtively to squeeze out his clothes.

" It's all ready," said Ann, who had a bright pink jersey over her red silk pyjamas. Sovra was heating some milk for the coffee Ann had made. She was wearing her old patched pyjamas of striped flannel, and a shapeless grey jersey over them.

"It's just about ready, Alastair," she said, turning round. "Ian, come on — what *have* you been doing?"

Ian stayed where he was. Water poured off him and collected in pools round his feet. His hair dripped, his face dripped, and when he moved everything dripped at once.

"I'm afraid I'm rather damp," he said, vaguely brushing at his shorts.

"Did you fall in?" asked Ann rather scornfully.

"Not exactly *fell*," said Ian. He seemed to be trying not to laugh.

"I threw him in," said Alastair briefly. "I thought it would do him good."

There was a moment of shocked silence, then Sovra suddenly started to giggle, and Ian joined her, and Alastair stopped looking tired and worried and laughed so much that he overbalanced and subsided onto one of the camp beds. Ann waited for them to recover, looking puzzled.

"Oh, Ian, go away and dry yourself," said Sovra weakly. "Oh dear, I wish I'd seen you."

"You don't object?" asked Alastair.

"I'm jolly glad. Ian, go *on*. You're making everything soaking wet."

Ian took his towel and pyjamas and went out. They heard him still giggling as he rubbed himself dry.

"I think you're all crackers," said Ann. "The supper will be spoiled if you don't come and eat it."

" Sorry, Ann," said Alastair.   " We Celtic types, you know."

" I didn't know Celtic meant giggling over nothing. Sovra, pour out that coffee. Where's the toast? Here's your fish, Alastair."

She dealt out the food in a businesslike way, and they set to work on the mackerel.

Ian came in with his hair on end, wearing pyjamas like Sovra's, only more patched.

" Here's your jersey," said Ann.   " I've done the elbows, but it's not frightfully beautiful."

" Och, I don't mind about frightful beauty. Thank you, Angelica. Sorry I was uncouth to you. I say, mackerel ! Sovra, move up."

He sat down beside Sovra on the bed, not looking at all sorry. However, Ann realized that he felt friendly towards her again, [and tried to feel kinder herself.

" You're a very good cook," said Alastair, trying to cheer her up.

" Mackerel are easy," she answered, but she looked pleased.

" Did you see lots of people ? " asked Sovra.

Alastair nodded, and the worried look came back to his eyes.

" I rather wish I'd never come. There's so much I could do here, and if it wasn't for this mortgage I could keep going and do a bit of farming, like my uncle. The people I saw were so friendly, they might have known me all my life. It would be a good feeling to belong here, not just come here on holiday."

" Oh, it *is* sad ! " said Sovra. " Have some toast. Buttered toast is so comforting."

He took some, and smiled.

" I didn't mean to be depressing," he said. " Shall we all go on an expedition tomorrow, if it's fine ? I needn't go home just yet. We could go across in your boat and see Donald. I promised I'd go again before I left."

They agreed eagerly, and spent the rest of the evening making plans and looking at the map Alastair had brought, while Ann thought about food for the next day and wondered whether she really wanted to go out in the boat again.

Next morning there was a brisk wind from the north, and the surface of the loch was wrinkled with cross-cross ripples and currents. Ann looked down at it from the cliffs and decided that she would rather stay ashore.

" I'd like to, honestly," she assured the others. " I'm longing to explore Fionn-ard. And I'll have a wizard time clearing up the mess in the shieling, with all you Celtic types out of the way."

She seemed to mean what she said, so the others agreed to leave her there, and set out with a picnic lunch and raincoats. Above the sea the sky was clear, but there were clouds inland, and the hills were distinct and bright, as if rain was in the air. The wind blew in cool gusts and smelt of grass and bracken.

They reached the top of the rock ladder, and Alastair suddenly exclaimed,

" I'm awfully sorry, but I don't think I shall be able to climb down. I never thought of that. You'll have to pick me up somewhere beyond the bog."

" Wait a bit," said Ian.   " Couldn't we let you down
with a rope ? "

" Yes, I expect so.   Have you got one ? "

" There's one in the boat.   Sovra, come and help
untie it.   It'll be quicker than rowing along to the
landing place."

They brought the mooring rope from the boat, and
Ann came to help, and Alastair was lowered down the
hole with the rope looped round his chest, holding on
to the steps in the rock and fending off with his good
foot.

" All right," he called up to the three at the top.
" I'm down."

They let go suddenly, and there was a muffled bump
from below.

" I was wrong," said Alastair.   " I'm down now.
Right down.   Someone come and take this heap of
rope off me."

The others scrambled down and found him lying flat
on his back with the rope on top, looking helpless but
rather amused.

Ian disentangled the rope and took it off to the boat,
while Sovra helped Alastair over the loose stones and
Ann climbed up again into the sunny hollow.

" It must be years since I was in here," said Alastair,
looking round the dim cave.   " There's the ring I fixed
in the rock, over there."

" Yes.   We use that to tie up the boat.   Did you have
to come in at high tide always, too ? "

Ian had come back to help them, and as he heard this
he suddenly cried out as if something had bitten him.

"Sovra! The tide! It won't be nearly high enough."

"Oh," said Sovra, trying to remember when they had last been out in the boat.

"It'll be high about three, I think," said Alastair. "But that doesn't matter, if you go straight out and don't take the side way."

"Straight out? Can we?"

"We came in that way first of all," said Sovra, "but we didn't mean to and we nearly got sunk."

"I used to do it often," said Alastair, limping to the edge of the water and looking at the waterfall that roared down beyond the cave. The noise drowned his words, but he pointed to the calmer water between the edge of the whirlpool and the sunken rocks, and nodded encouragingly.

"All right," shouted Ian. "We can both swim, anyway."

Alastair climbed into the boat and swung himself neatly along to the stern. He sat down and took one of the oars to fend off from the rock. The others got in and stowed the food under their raincoats in the bows, with the mooring rope coiled round them. Ian pushed off with the second oar, and Sovra sat on the rope to guide them out.

The boat grated off the sloping pebbles and swung round in the shallow water until the bows pointed at the waterfall. Ian and Alastair rowed slowly, pausing between strokes to see where they were going. The boat edged along by the sunken reef, jerking as it was pulled by the currents racing round the foot of the waterfall.

The spray drifted over, cold and clinging, but soon the warmth of the sun struck through it and dazzled the three in the boat after the gloom of the cave.

" Look out ! " cried Sovra suddenly, but she was too late. A wave came swinging round the circle of the whirlpool, and hit the boat under the chin so that it reared up and tilted sideways. Sovra collapsed backwards, and Ian fell on his face on top of his oar, and the boat spun to the left and hovered for a moment before the current took it.

Alastair shipped his oar as quick as lightning, and twisted round, leaning out over the stern. The sunken rock was still just in reach, only a foot or so below the surface, and he managed to get a grip on its rough spine. The inward movement of the boat was checked, and the bows swung right round until they pointed at the cave. Alastair hooked his left leg under the seat and leaned further out, pulling on the rock with both hands. The boat resisted at first, for the current was urging it towards the shore. Soon, however, Alastair felt it moving reluctantly, and the strain on his arms eased a little. He moved one hand along, and the other after it, and slowly the heavy boat gathered way and slid along the rock out of the current and into safe waters.

Sovra was up again by this time, and had straightened out Ian and the oars. Ian seized the rowlock Alastair had been using, and slammed it into place opposite his own. Using both oars he pulled his hardest, and in three strokes the boat was right away from the waterfall and quivering gently to the ripples out on Loch Fionn.

Ian shipped the oars, and turned to help Alastair get the right way up again.

"You saved us from a watery doom," said Sovra breathlessly.

"I *am* a fool," said Ian. "I always fall over at the wrong moment."

Alastair unhooked his leg and pulled himself round, completely out of breath. Water dripped off his hair and face, where the sea had splashed up against the boat, and strands of seaweed were twined round his wet arms.

"Perhaps I oughtn't to have taken you out that way," he said when his breath had come back. "I'd forgotten what it was like."

"Och, it was thrilling," said Ian. "But how did you haul us along? The boat must weigh half a ton."

"You must be awfully strong. Throwing Ian in the lochan, and pulling the boat along like that," said Sovra. "Did you hurt yourself, though? That rock's horribly sharp."

"Most of my skin's still there," said Alastair, examining his hands.

"We're always so stupid," said Ian, full of remorse as he saw how Alastair's fingers were bleeding. "Sovra never sees things in time——"

"And when I do tell him to look out, he just falls flat and helpless like a jellyfish," said Sovra indignantly.

"You seem to survive, somehow, in spite of your stupidity," said Alastair. "Shall I take an oar again, Ian?"

"No, I'll do a bit on my own, just to show Sovra I'm

not always a jellyfish. You know, if we were cleverer, we wouldn't be here at all."

" We jolly nearly aren't," said Sovra, still feeling shuddery inside. " If it wasn't for Alastair. . . ."

" What do you mean ? " Alastair asked.

" Well, we came across to Fionn-ard first without meaning to at all, because we didn't look where we were going. Then we burnt down our bothy at home, so we had to go and explore for a camping place, and then we went too near the waterfall and got swished into the cave. If we hadn't been so stupid about the bothy, we'd still be in it now. We mightn't ever have found the shieling."

" And I wouldn't have come up here again," said Alastair, interested.

" Och, you said all that last night," said Sovra. " Stop talking, Ian, and get a move on. The wind's pushing us back all the time."

" Ann, now," Ian went on, taking no notice of her. " She's clever. She'd never go and stumble into things by accident."

" I like Ann," said Sovra, " but in a way I'm glad she's not here. She does fuss a bit, though it's nice having someone who likes cooking."

" Well, you can't eat your cake at both ends," said Ian. " Alastair, do you want something to tie round your hand ? "

" It's the sort of cut you can hardly see but won't stop bleeding," said Alastair, sucking his left hand. " If you have got a spare handkerchief——"

" There's a scarf in here," said Sovra, and pulled the

haversack out from behind the pile of rope. "It's Ann's. She'll not mind. Oh, and here's the bit of newspaper that talked about Kindrachill."

Alastair wrapped the scarf tightly round his hand, and read the piece of newspaper, which was now rather crumpled. He frowned as he read about Kindrachill, and turned to the advertisements on the other side to take his mind off it. Ian watched him, and frowned in sympathy, and thought that perhaps if he *was* clever he could find a way to stop Kindrachill being sold.

"I say, we're getting blown right over into the sound," said Sovra, when they had gone about half-way across the loch.

"A bit of port drift," agreed Alastair.

"I thought it was awful hard work," said Ian, glancing over his shoulder. "We'll never make Donald's house at this rate."

"I'll take an oar," said Alastair. "Sovra, come and sit in the stern, It's easier with the bows empty."

"Can you row?" asked Sovra doubtfully, as she climbed past Ian.

"I don't row with my feet. Keep us heading for Donald, will you?"

The boat moved faster as the two oarsmen pulled, but although they kept the bows pointing at the little grey house ahead, the whole boat was carried sideways continually by the wind.

"D'you know where we *are* going?" remarked Sovra after a while.

"America, I should think, unless Ireland gets in the way," said Alastair, looking round.

" Oho," said Ian. " Castle Island. Just look. I knew we'd get there one day when we were trying hard not to. Like Alice in the Red Queen's Garden."

" Castle Island ? "

" It's really Eilean Glas, but we've always thought it looked like a castle," Sovra explained.

" Do let's go there now. We'll never get across to Donald in this wind," said Ian.

" All right," said Alastair. " I've never been to it either. Pull us round a bit, Ian."

They changed course and made for Castle Island, due west of them. The wind helped them now, and soon they were close enough to see the harebells and sea-pinks growing on the rocks, and the seaweed lifting on the waves as they broke on the shore.

" Let's land on the southern end," said Alastair. " Then the wind will keep the boat off the rocks when it's moored."

They found a landing place where the rock ran out into the sea and protected a stony beach. When they were all ashore with their haversacks and raincoats, Ian pushed the boat out into deeper water, while Alastair made the end of the mooring rope fast round a big boulder.

" Do a good knot," said Sovra, watching him. " We don't want to be marooned."

" That's all right," he said. " Now let's see what the island's like."

He found a piece of driftwood to use as a walking-stick, and the three explorers climbed up to the top of the square lump of rock that looked like a castle. The

island was small and bare, with one or two patches of
grass in sheltered hollows among the rocks, and ferns and
harebells and heather clinging to the cracks and ledges
on the bare rock faces.

" I say, you can see a lot," said Ian, as they reached
the top and stood to look at the view.

Castle Island lay at the mouth of Loch Fionn, and
from it you could see the wilderness of islands, and
beyond the islands the darker blue of the open sea.
The clearness of the rain-filled air made every rock and
precipice stand out sharp and black ; you could count
the boulders for twenty miles around. Ian and Sovra
had never been out as far as this before. Behind them lay
the loch, and Ben Shian cloudy dark ; on their right was
the familiar coastline curving round towards Melvick,
and on their left lay the western point of Fionn-ard,
with the singing sands just visible beyond the spur of
rock.

Ian looked at the singing sands, and then looked hard
again in the same direction. Then he turned to the
others, and said casually,

" Don't be alarmed, but a slight awfulness has happened."

" Ian ! " cried Sovra, who knew that when he talked
like that it was usually a very big awfulness. " What
do you mean ? "

" There's the boat," he said, and pointed to a black
object lilting away on the waves, being carried by the
wind and tide towards the distant singing sands. It
was already a long way from the island. The ripples
bounced it gaily and tilted it from side to side, and the

wind came in gusts against the broad stern and pushed it gently along towards the outermost point of Fionn-ard.

The island suddenly felt small and lonely ; a bare lump of rock miles from anywhere ; and the three standing on it looked vainly round for any sign of another boat on the sea or a house on the land where there might be people watching. Donald's cottage was the only one in sight, and it had no window looking on the sea.

" How on earth did it get loose ? " cried Sovra, after the first wild stare all round. " Alastair, you tied it up."

" I did," said Alastair. " It can't have broken the rope."

" Let's go and see," said Ian, and led the way down to the little beach where they had landed.

There was the boulder where Alastair had fastened the rope, and there was one end of the rope still securely tied round it. The other end was floating loose on the water.

" My sorrow ! " exclaimed Ian. " We never tied the other end onto the boat again. Aren't we *daft !* "

" Well, we really have done it this time," said Sovra. " No boats ever come this way."

" Singing sands are nearest," said Ian. " I wonder if I——"

" No, of course you couldn't swim as far as that," said Alastair sharply. " I could have done it once, but not now."

He scowled down at his bad foot, and sat on a rock to think what should be done. The other two sat down and thought with him. Sovra gazed at the trailing rope and felt cross at the way they could never manage to do anything quite right. They had been so careful about tying up the shore end of the rope, and all the time the other end was free, just waiting to slip over the stern as the wind carried the boat out beyond its length.

Ian looked up at the square-cut rock behind them, and his thoughts wandered.

" Did you know," he said presently, " that every Sultan of Zanzibar has to build himself a new palace ? "

The others hardly heard him. Sovra was wondering how many days their sandwiches would last, and Alastair was so annoyed by his own carelessness that he would not trust himself to speak. At last, however, he made an effort and said cheerfully,

" Well, we've had the boat. It must be past Fionnard by now. So let's consider what to do."

" We might wave things from the top, in case there's someone looking," said Sovra.

" Let's have our dinner, anyway," said Ian. " Or do you think we ought to keep it, in case we're not rescued for days ? "

" Somebody's bound to see us soon," said Alastair, though he was not as confident as he sounded. " How soon will your parents miss you ? "

" As soon as they don't get a message from us," said Ian. " But Ann had a message to take today, so it won't be till tomorrow evening."

" Ann will know something's happened to us," said Sovra.

" Yes, but she might think we'd decided to stay with Donald, or something daft like that," said Ian. " Look at the way she ran off and left me, when I was lying unconscious with the sea coming up all over me."

"Och, be quiet. Alastair, can't you think of anything?"

"Yes, of course," he said, getting up eagerly. "We must light a fire. There's plenty of driftwood. Someone's bound to notice the smoke."

"What a marvellous idea!" cried Ian. "Let's eat our sandwiches, then."

Sovra insisted on keeping back some of the food, just in case, but they ate the rest straight away, and then set about collecting firewood.

"This ought to burn all right," said Alastair, laying the smallest pieces of wood across a bunch of dead heather and dry grass.

"What about matches?" said Sovra, her heart suddenly sinking. "Ian, have you any?"

Ian felt in his pockets, and produced a clasp-knife.

"That's all I've got," he said. "If we had a horse, I could take stones out of its hooves. I don't have any matches though."

"Don't panic," said Alastair, searching his pockets. "I've got some somewhere, I know . . . Here they are."

The fire was soon blazing up into the wind, for driftwood is the best kindling there is, in spite of soaking in sea-water for so long. The smoke whirled round as the gusts caught it, and rose in a satisfying thick smudge that would be visible for miles.

"It's really rather exciting," said Sovra, watching the smoke. "I've never been marooned before."

" Well, you are now," said Ian.   " We've been nearly burnt and nearly drowned, and now we're going to be nearly starved.   In some places they eat seaweed, don't they.   It doesn't look very nice."

" We need some more firewood," said Alastair. " You can eat your seaweed later on."

Ian grinned at him and went off obediently to look for driftwood, going along the outer shore of the island. There were heaps of seaweed all along the shore, driven up by winds and waves into the hollows among the rocks. Tangled in the seaweed were all kinds of things ; branches and twigs and planks and barrel-staves, orange skin and broken fragments of china, and one or two of the green glass floats from fishing nets.   Ian soon had both arms full of driftwood, and turned towards the grass above the rocks, where it would be easier to walk back to the fire.

There was a little patch of sand below the grass, smoothed by the last high tide and sparkling with shells. Ian crossed it, making for the easiest way up onto the grassy bank.   The shells were bright and fascinating, and he walked slowly to try and count their colours ; orange and yellow and purple and crimson and white and grey and palest pink, too many to remember afterwards.

As he reached the edge of the grass he suddenly noticed something else, something brighter than the shells, lying at his feet in an empty patch of sand.   For a moment he stood still and stared.   It was a green and gold dragon, with fiery red eyes and tongue, wonderfully scaly and lifelike.

" The lost brooch," thought Ian, his mind flashing swiftly. " Six hundred pounds reward! If we had that we could buy a motor-boat and go for miles, and proper fishing rods, and cameras——"

But before he had thought for a second, he knew what he really wanted to do with those six hundred pounds. He glanced quickly round, and saw Alastair following him. He had turned in towards the sand, and was walking carefully over the rough rocks without looking up.

Ian went on quickly with his load, and reached the fire before stopping to look round. Sovra was kneeling by the leaping flame, hitting the burning wood to make the sparks fly. She turned to watch Alastair, and as they both looked they saw how he limped slowly across the sand and came to a standstill on the edge of the grass.

After a moment's pause he stooped and picked something up, and Ian smiled and turned to put more wood on the fire. Alastair came back along the grass with one hand in his pocket, and Sovra noticed that his eyes were shining.

" Ian," he said, not quite smiling. " Can you guess what I have here ? "

He took his hand out of his pocket, and held it out, closed over something.

" Why would I be able to ? " asked Ian innocently. He wanted Alastair to feel that the reward was truly his own ; that he had been the only one to see the brooch.

" What have you found ? " cried Sovra.

" Can you really not guess, Ian ? "

Ian shook his head, and Alastair opened his hand and showed the glittering green and gold dragon, flashing in the rain-clear light.

" Kindrachill," he said.

13. Welcome Home

ANN SPENT SOME TIME, after the others had gone, in clearing up the shieling. When she had hung up all the coats and tidied the beds and stacked the crockery and piled up the books, and had pushed everything else into the cupboard and shut it in, she looked round with satisfaction and felt as if the house belonged to her.

Next she decided to take the message to the post-box, and when this was done she was free to amuse herself. Somehow it was not at all boring to be alone on Fionnard. She explored the shore below the deserted village, and then along the top of the cliffs until she reached the bay of the singing sands. The tide was coming in, but there was still a wide stretch of sand above the water ; much more than when she had come there with the others. The shells lay in curving lines where the last tide had stranded them, and Ann thought she would climb down and collect some for her mother. She found the way down, and was soon lying on the sand in the shelter of the rocks, kicking her legs idly and scooping up the warm shells and pebbles in both hands. The clouds were spreading across the sky, but had not reached the sun, and out of the wind it was warm and peaceful. The waves surged and splashed and bubbled,

and it was a long time before Ann looked up sleepily
and gazed out to sea.

For a moment she saw nothing but the dazzling brightness of foam and sun and white sand, but as her eyes
became used to the brilliance she saw a boat, large
as life and twice as mysterious; lonely and empty,
drifting across the mouth of the little bay.

" It's their boat ! " Ann exclaimed, and sat up
quickly. " What on earth's happened ? "

The boat lilted a little on the incoming waves, and
slipped sideways, into the shelter of the rocky point.
With the wind no longer pushing it, and the swell
rolling under it towards the shore, it glided gently in
until it reached the far side of the bay.   Here it lingered,
sidling up against the rock as if it was trying to make up
its mind where to go, in towards the sand or round the
point and across Loch Drachill.

Ann jumped up and ran for the cliff, and climbed up
as fast as she could.   From the top of the ridge she gazed
across Loch Fionn, searching for some sign of the others,
and wondering where on earth they could be.   She
looked and looked, and was just giving it up when she
saw a smudge of smoke going up from the island out in
the mouth of the loch.

" Oh no," she said.   " Oh, how absolutely drab.
How completely grim.   They're marooned.   It must
be them on that island.   Oh dear, they're marooned and
the boat's come across to me, and what can *I* do ? "

She looked down at the boat, which was dipping on
the waves and seemed to say,

" Get in and row across to that island."

" Oh, I can't possibly ! " said Ann. " It's much too far. Besides, I'm no good on the sea."

" Hurry up," said the boat. " I can't wait all day," and it nosed against the rock as if it wanted to be off into Loch Drachill.

" Oh help," said Ann, giving one last desperate look round, but there was no help within reach, and the smoke on the island was thicker, and plainly a signal of distress. The sea was choppy, but not too rough to row through single-handed, and the wind had dropped. It was the sort of thing you couldn't get out of, however seasick you were likely to be.

Ann took a deep breath and climbed rapidly down again, and ran out across the rocks to the boat.

" Of course I can do it," she told herself. " If Sovra can row all by herself, I can. I'm older than her and more sensible. Besides, I ve been sailing."

Comforted by these thoughts, she got into the boat and took the oars, and pushed off into deep water. The oars seemed heavy and awkward at first, and she was glad that nobody was there to see her. However, before she was out of the bay she had discovered how to keep the oars moving together, and soon she was striking out lustily for Castle Island. Fionn-ard drew away and grew smaller, and the island began to loom a little larger when she glanced over her shoulder, and soon she knew she couldn't turn back, for the mainland was too far away.

The three shipwrecked explorers had found a sheltered place near their fire, where they could watch Loch Fionn for any signs of a rescue. Ian and Sovra were much too excited about Kindrachill to feel anxious about being marooned, and talked as hard as they could go.   Alastair took no notice of them.   He felt rather dazed by the sudden change in his fortunes, and had to keep looking at the brooch to make sure it was real.

After a while Ian and Sovra calmed down a little, and Alastair got up and flung more wood on the fire, and then lay back in a clump of heather and stretched his arms luxuriously.

" This *is* a good show," he said.   " I'm glad I came here.   I was going to give it up and forget Kindrachill existed, but it would have been pretty grim.   I never realized how much I liked the place until I came up here again."

" Oh, it's too thrilling to bear ! " said Sovra, jumping up quickly.   " I'm going to look out over the other side."

" Sovra's always so energetic," said Ian, as she climbed up the rock behind them.

" So is Ann.   Girls often are," said Alastair.

" Ann's different, though.   I'm the one that thinks of things, and Ann knows how to do them, and Sovra goes and does them.   I suppose that's what Daddy means when he talks about division of labour."

" Not much labour about your share ! "

A loud shout behind them cut short their conversation, and they got up, to find Sovra leaping about on the top of the rock, waving her arms.

" Saved ! " she cried.   " A sail !   A sail ! "

" I don't see any sail," said Ian, joining her.

" Och, you snaggle-tooth, I mean a boat !   There, look."

" Good old Annabella," said Ian, waving.   " All by

herself, and it's quite a rough sea. She's braver than I thought."

Ann looked round when she heard them calling, and shouted back triumphantly, though it was rather a feeble shout. She was almost breathless with the struggle against the waves, and her arms and shoulders were aching, but she managed to bring the boat swiftly along and into the sheltered water by the little beach, where the three castaways were waiting for her.

They set off again straight away for Camas Ban, so that Alastair could telephone to the people who had lost the brooch, and to his lawyer in Glasgow. By the time they had told Ann about the mooring rope, and the fire, and the brooch turning up like magic to save Kindrachill, and had all said how brave she was, the tide had brought them nearly home, and Ann was feeling pleasantly like a heroine.

They moored the boat at Camas Ban, making sure that both ends of the rope were fastened, and then they went up to the house all singing at the top of their voices, so that everyone came rushing out to see what on earth was happening.

"They're all daft," said Mrs. Kennedy faintly. "Look at them."

They were certainly not very tidy. The wind had tangled Sovra's hair and unravelled Ann's plaits, and spray had splashed over all of them, and blown ashes from the fire were mixed streakily in with the spray, and Alastair looked worse than any of them, with his walking-stick of driftwood and a bloodstained scarf wound about his hand.

Dr. Kennedy listened to the incoherent surge of words that greeted him, and quickly realized what it was all about. In a few minutes Alastair was settled in an arm-chair in the sitting-room, one hand on the telephone and the other having sticking plaster put on it by Mrs. Kennedy, and the other three were waiting on the grass outside, eating bread and jam as if they had been marooned for days without food.

After some time Alastair came out to them, looking clean and very pleased.

" It's all right," he said. " Everything's fixed now. Give me some of that bread, Sovra."

" Oh, how hectically wizard ! " cried Ann. " How super. How wiz-*biz* ! "

She clapped her hands and looked so excited that her mother wouldn't have recognized her.

" You see, now," said Sovra. " It really *is* ' Welcome home ', whatever Ian says."

" Donald will be pleased," said Ian.

" It's a good show all round," said Alastair, eating bread and jam. " I'll have to get back to Glasgow as soon as I can, though. I'll collect my things from the shieling straight away. I hope I'll be able to come back to Kindrachill in a few days when all the legal stuff is settled. You must come and visit me there."

He turned to look at Ben Shian, and the distant cliffs of Fionn-ard, and suddenly smiled and looked as excited as Ann.

" I can hardly believe I'll be coming back for good," he said. " Good-bye until I do, anyway."

When he had gone, the wind rose again, and the mist

came drifting from the north, covering the mountains, and the others rowed back across the loch as fast as they could, to get to the shieling before the rain began.

" Oh, how exciting it all is," sighed Ann. " I never dreamed of anything like this happening up here. I thought it would be frightfully boring."

" Stay with us and you won't be bored," said Sovra. " You may be seasick or shipwrecked or drowned or lost or starved or burned or killed by falling over a cliff, but you won't be bored."

" I wonder what will happen to us next," said Ian thoughtfully.

He found out when he reached the shieling. Alastair had taken all his belongings, but there was a note on the table, weighted with a lump of butter that happened to be lying about loose.

" It's for you, Ian," said Ann, hurrying to tidy away the butter.

He read it, and his eyes widened and he went very red and said, " My sorrow ! " several times, until the other two shouted at him impatiently and demanded to know what it said.

" He's given me the shieling," said Ian breathlessly. " To keep for ever. Fair exchange, he says."

" Why on earth does he say that ? " asked Sovra, looking admiringly at the untidy signature.

" I suppose he saw me stop and look at the brooch and not pick it up."

" You saw it first ? "

" Yes. I didn't want him to know I'd found it too, in case he thought twice about taking the reward."

" He didn't think twice," said Ann.

" No. I suppose he realized why I left it lying there, and he wasn't going to spoil a good deed like that."

" Don't try and sound noble," said Sovra. " You wanted him to have Kindrachill more than anything."

" Well, as much as anything," said Ian, trying to be honest. " Anyway, he's given me the shieling because of it. Isn't it thrilling ! "

He started a Highland fling, and nearly knocked Ann into the fire, where she was seeing about the kettle she had left on the embers.

" Oh, stop it ! " she cried. " Go outside if you must leap about. Sovra, take him away."

She pushed him over to the door, kindly but firmly.

" Let's go up on the hill and look at the islands," Sovra suggested.

" Oh dear, the kettle's going to boil over," cried Ann, and rushed back to rescue it.

The others ran up onto the ridge to look out to sea. The rain was sweeping down towards them like swaying grey curtains, chasing the golden light that gleamed beyond the islands. There was a cold blue lustre on the water, and the wind was sharp with spray.

Ian turned, with the salt stinging his cheek and the wind in his hair, and looked down at the shieling, sheltered among the trees. He felt a great satisfaction at the sight of it. He and Sovra might be rather stupid, and mess things up more than people like Ann, who would never let a kettle boil over. But on the whole he couldn't help feeling they'd not done too badly.